USA TODAY BESTSELLING AUTHOR

MEGHAN QUINN

THE MODERN GENTLEMAN

Published by Hot-Lanta Publishing, LLC

Copyright 2020

Cover Design By: RBA Designs

PROLOGUE

Dear Gents,

See that remote in your hand? Yeah, the one that's covered in pizza sauce and last night's Buffalo wings? I want you to take a good look at it. Do you have it memorized? Good, now bend at the waist, set it on the coffee table, and stand up. Don't you dare look at that remote again, don't even glance at it. And the Xbox that's calling your name, go ahead and forget about that as well, because guess what? You're starting a new journey and it doesn't include television, video games, or high-fiving over a bubbly belch from the bowels of your intestinal tract. Forget everything you've ever known about being a man, forget the hall passes you have for being a man, and forget every natural instinct you carry inside your bones. Because I'm here to refine you, replenish your knowledge on the male species, and turn you into a modern gentleman: a well-respected, polished, and confident individual with an epic sex appeal and killer style that will woo any female with a simple flash of your honest charm.

Stick with me, gents. I'm starting a revolution and it begins with you.

Sincerely,

The Modern Gentleman

CHAPTER ONE

WES

"Dude, you're drinking a Mang-O-Rita."

I stare at the can in my hand and shamelessly nod. Yup, I am. I'm also wearing cut-off sweatpants and a neon orange Hawaiian shirt I wore once for a destination wedding in Hawaii. It's a far cry from my usual impeccably tailored suit and tie.

Caden, my best friend, continues, "It's not even a Lime-A-Rita. It's mango, chick-flavored piss-water, man."

Don't I fucking know it.

It's without a doubt, a chick drink, and yet, it's the only thing I have left of *her*.

"And what's with the lady scarf?"

Ehh, okay, so I have her scarf too. I found it in my hall closet and sniffed it for about an hour and a half last night while I tipped a carton of cold lo mein noodles into my mouth for dinner. Sniff, tip, sniff, tip. It was a process I repeated until I was out of noodles. And then I proceeded to pick the missed noodles off the floor and eat those as well. Can you see where this is going? I'm a hot mess.

"And why is the scarf wrapped around your head?"

Because that's how she would wear it . . .

"My head was cold." I stick my chin up in the air. Yes, good answer.

"And the Joni Mitchell playing in the background? *Clouds and illusions?* What kind of crap is that?"

Depressing, that's what it is. It's depressing crap. But I can't help but sniff the tail end of the scarf wrapped around my head, hold my lady can to my chest, and sway . . . fucking sway.

"I really don't know love at all . . ." I sing softly with my head tilted to the sky, memories of the woman I love floating through my mind.

I miss—

A pillow whips me in the face, dislodging my headscarf and making me spill my lady drink all over my offensively colored Hawaiian shirt.

"What the hell?" I hold the dripping can away from me and sit up on my couch, just as Caden sits next to me.

"Dude, you need to get your shit together." Caden looks around my apartment. "When was the last time you cleaned in here? It smells like rotten goat cheese with a touch"—he sniffs the air—"of Doritos." Maybe because I was crushing Doritos in my palm last night, letting the tortilla shards indent my palm, anything to take away some of the pain in my heart. They didn't do the trick. "I leave town for a few days and this is what I come back to? An unshaved, stanky version of The Modern Gentleman. What the hell happened?"

Everything. Everything that was not supposed to happen happened. And I should have known it would pan out like this. Anyone reading my column could have easily guessed the outcome of my future, the outcome of my "experiment." Most of them probably tuned in every week and laughed at my words, saying, "Oh this is going to backfire, this is going to backfire sooo badly."

It did. Oh boy, did it backfire.

Meeting someone over a pile of dog crap doesn't necessarily

scream, "This is the start of the world's most epic romance." Yup . . . should've known.

Dog doo-doo. You read that correctly. I met the love of my life over dog doo-doo.

And I lost her because of my boss's "brilliant" idea he proposed to me to "amp up" my column.

I sigh and take another sip of the piss-water. "She broke up with me, man."

His eyes widen and he opens his mouth briefly, then shuts it, considering how he wants to approach this conversation. I know what he really wants to say. Cringing, he finally asks, "Did she find out?"

I nod, knowing what's coming next. "Yup. And if you say, 'I told you so,' I'm going to knock your nuts off your body."

He smirks. "What about I warned you?"

"Same fucking thing." I slouch on the sofa, regretting every decision I made over the past two months.

We sit in silence, the weight of my loss hanging heavily in the room. She wasn't just special to me; she was special to my group of friends. She exuded a bright, fun, innocent energy no one could resist, especially Caden, who told me so many times to come clean, to tell her what I was doing. But I was scared of losing my damn job.

Fuck, I was scared of losing her.

And oh the power of hindsight, because *that fear was completely valid*. Caden folds his hands in his lap and exhales.

"Seems like you only have one option left. You have to get her back."

I shake my head. Not going to happen. "She specifically told me to crawl into my own scrotum and drown in my sperm. I'm pretty positive when a girl wants my unborn children to kill me, she's not going to want to talk to me again."

"So you're going to give up? That's not very *Modern Gentleman* of you. Tell me, what would he do right now?" Caden gives me a once-over. "He sure as hell wouldn't be wearing a scarf around his head and listening to Joni Mitchell."

No, no, he would not. Fucking Modern Gentleman persona.

Resigned, I say, "The Modern Gentleman wouldn't have taken such a dishonest job from his boss in the first place. God, this entire experiment is the antithesis of what The Modern Gentleman would have done. I'm a freaking oxymoron." I finish up my drink. "No . . . I'm just a moron."

"I'm not going to argue with that." Caden perks up and looks at me, hands still folded. "But, dude. This"—he waves his hand over my pathetic self—"*needs* her back in your life. What you've got going on right now isn't working."

"I know." I sit up as well and run my hands over my face. "She's impossible to get in touch with though, so how the hell am I going to fix this?"

Caden pats my shoulder with a smile. "With some old-fashioned wooing, bro. Your modern ways aren't going to work with this girl."

Isn't that the statement of the year? My modern ways never worked with her. She's a rare breed, the type of girl who comes around once in a lifetime, a woman so damn perfect for me that all I can do is hope and pray I can earn her respect, proving I am the right man for her. *The only man for her.*

What happened you ask? Dying to know?

Well, I'm going to tell you, from the very beginning, and you're going to want to scream and say, this isn't going to end well. Let's all take a moment and say, "Wes, you're an idiot."

Good?

Perfect.

Now that we've got that out of the way, here's how it all went down . . .

CHAPTER TWO

D ear Modern Gentleman,
    I've recently been given the opportunity to reinvent myself.
Without going into details about my past, I want to drop the nerdy persona
that's stuck with me since middle school and transform myself into the
epitome of The Modern Gentleman. The problem is, I'm having a hard
time staying out of the friend zone. Any guidance would be appreciated.
    Sincerely,
    Permanent Friend

Dear Permanent Friend,
While you're busy switching from Reeboks to your very own pair of Stuart
Weitzmans, there is a general rule of thumb you need to remember when
interacting with the opposite sex. Brand this motto on your soul: a
gentleman on the streets, an alpha in the sheets. What does that mean? Hold
the door open for your girl, but when she passes through, give that ass a
gentle slap. Let it be known you are every bit the upstanding man she
dreams of but you will ravish the hell out of her when you get home.
Good luck, Gent,
The Modern Gentleman

WES

TWO MONTHS EARLIER

"Let me get that for you." I jog to the glass door that leads into the offices of HYPE, the leading news and social media company in the country.

"Thank you, Wes. You're so sweet."

"My pleasure." I nod at Mary, the mother hen of the office, as she walks through the door, holding her morning coffee from the seventh floor. We're on the thirty-third floor, but she insists the best coffee in New York City is on the seventh floor of our building. We don't own the seventh. It's full of accountants, but according to Mary, the people with the numbers make the best coffee. I don't dare fight her over it.

With my very own coffee in hand—black from the local café around the corner—I pass reception and greet Esmerelda with a wave, since she's already fielding a slew of phone calls. She smiles politely and finger-waves back.

"Wes, man. Catch the game last night?" Terrance asks as he passes me in the hallway.

"Yanks killed it, man. That rookie is giving the AL a run for their money. I'd be surprised if we're not eating hot dogs this Fall."

As I make my way down the hallway toward my office, I greet everyone by name.

"Dalilah, is that a new dress?"

"Jo, how's Danny? Is he over the pox yet?"

"Rose, please tell me you left more of those heavenly brownies in the break room."

If you learn anything from me, let it be this: get to know the people around you. You never know whose day you might brighten by remembering a small tidbit about their life.

I walk through my morning routine, making the rounds, engaging in small talk, straightening out crooked ties, and handing out quick winks to those who catch my eye. When I reach my office, Caden meets me at the door, his tablet in hand, and an annoyed look on his face. The man is a workaholic, has zero time for anything outside of the office, and should be on the fast track to Chief Operating Officer. But Frank Bellaton, our current COO, has to retire before that happens. So for now, Caden works his ass off with very little acknowledgment.

"What's got your brow all busted today?" I ask in greeting.

Eyes fixed on the tablet in front of him, he doesn't even look at me when he answers, "Frank called for a creative meeting this morning. He had another dream last night."

"Oh Jesus." I try to hold back the eye-roll that comes with mention of Frank's dreams, but it's damn near impossible. "Who's going to be the sorry soul he picks on this time?"

"Who knows? No one's safe. Remember when he made Jennifer redo all her quizzes because he had a dream they should be in a circular format rather than square?"

"Took weeks off her life."

"Exactly." Caden shakes his head. "He should let the directors deal with content and focus on running the damn company."

Frank is not a reliable leader, but he has the occasional flash of brilliance, which is why the board of directors keep him around. Too bad they know nothing about his "dreams."

Whenever he comes into the office with a starry-eyed look, wearing his purple crushed-velvet jacket and gold shoes, you know he's about to turn someone's job upside down. And change is the nature of our jobs. As the leading source for news, entertainment, lifestyle, and mindless quizzes that tell you what Disney Princess you most resemble with five simple questions, we are constantly evolving to meet our readers' demands. Thankfully, my advice column, which helps dudes transform themselves into gentlemen of class and sex appeal, never changes. Guys ask questions, I answer them. Simple, popular, and makes me a damn good paycheck.

"When's the meeting?" I walk into my office and fire up my computer.

"Five minutes."

"Fun." I don't bother taking a seat at my desk. Instead, I snag my own tablet for notetaking, coffee still in hand. I'm going to need it. Frank likes to take his time during these meetings. "Want to head over to the conference room?"

"Yup, just waiting on you." Caden still has his head buried in his tablet as we step out of my office, but he maneuvers around the halls like a god, never running into anything.

"Hear from Roman this morning?" I ask, pausing to sip my coffee.

"No, but I heard from him last night."

"You got a call too?"

Caden chuckles. "Pretty sure everyone in Manhattan got a call from him last night. What did he say?" Caden lifts his head for a second, squinting as he tries to remember. "Something about six shots with fire inside of them."

"That's his new favorite shot, a B-52. Irish cream, Kahlua, and Triple sec. He had six? Hell, when he called me he was only up to four."

"Should I be offended that he always calls you first? I feel like I'm an afterthought after he's fucking ripped."

I chuckle and pat Caden on the back as we make our way down the hall. "Dude, you don't want to talk to him six shots in. He's way too emotional. You get fun Roman when he says whatever is on his mind. I get Roman who can't stop crying into the phone."

"He doesn't cry, does he?" Caden chuckles.

"Practically."

And speak of the devil. When we turn the corner into the conference room, Roman is sitting toward the back of the table, sunglasses on, a white button-up shirt barely buttoned, slightly crinkled, and his signature black hair askew. There's no way he went home last night—his usual five o'clock shadow looks like a full-on beard.

He's leaning his head into his hand, which is resting on the table next to him, the very picture of an eager employee, obviously. He groans and rubs his temple as we approach. Death consumes him. It's hard not to notice.

"Fun night?" I ask, the sound of my tablet smacking the table, making Roman cringe. Caden and I take our seats, preparing ourselves for what we know is going to be another drunk story from Roman.

He lets out a long breath and stares straight ahead. "Love Swipe got the best of me, man." I roll my eyes at the mention of Love Swipe, the premier dating app used in NYC right now. "I swiped right and wound up in crazy town with a busty blonde whose favorite pastime is sucking toes. I can't even look, I'm too scared." He holds his foot out under the conference table. "Take my shoe off. Do I still have fucking toenails? For the love of God, just give it to me straight. I need to know."

I slap his foot away. "Roman, self-respect man. You look like shit, and you're at work. Frank is going to fire your ass if you don't get it together."

Roman tips his glasses down and looks me dead in the eyes. "I'm not kidding when I say I walked on my heels all the way here. That lady did some serious damage. I don't think there's anything attached to my toes right now. I feel them bleeding as we speak."

"We'll deal with your toes later." I look at my watch and swat him in the stomach. "Sit up straight, button your damn shirt properly, and tuck it all the way in. And take off those sunglasses. You're on Frank's last nerve as it is, you don't need to give him an excuse to fire you."

The only reason Frank hasn't fired Roman yet is because he's damn good at his job. He's Vice President of Marketing and despite his inability to act like an adult, he's able to pull it together enough to head a well-oiled machine and keep us in the black every year. And he knows the ins and outs of the entire company better than anyone, even hung over four out of the five days he's at work.

"Promise you'll check my toes?"

"Christ." I adjust my watch. "Yes, just get it together. I've taught you better. Did you have your hangover drink this morning?"

Busy tucking in his shirt, he answers, "Dude, I still have that blonde's underwear in my back pocket. There was no way I was able to down a hangover drink before I got here. The only reason I didn't pass out at my desk this morning was because Polly guided me to the conference room and handed me coffee."

Polly, Roman's assistant, is another reason he hasn't been fired yet. She covers his ass every damn day and deserves every cent of her hefty yearly bonus.

Before I can answer, people start to filter in through the door, followed by Frank, who shuts us all in. Roman visibly straightens in his chair and acts like the professional he is . . . or pretends to be.

"Good morning." Frank stands tall and buttons his ubiquitous purple jacket. He scans the room. His goatee is longer than it should be and his eyebrows entirely too thin—there's certain facial hair etiquette men should follow, which Frank clearly refuses to acknowledge. As he adjusts his cufflinks, he asks, "How was everyone's weekend?"

Not giving anyone a chance to answer, he claps his hands together and starts pacing. He doesn't pace the width of the room, though. He takes laps around the conference table, his hand hovering over our heads like some kind of grown-up version of Duck, Duck, Goose. When he stops behind you, buckle up, because your work life is about to be "blessed" with one of his asinine ideas.

"I've been doing a lot of thinking about our social media presence and I think we're missing out on something." Oh boy. Here we go . . . He stops behind Caden and grips his shoulders while looking out over all of us. The tension in Caden's shoulders is entirely too noticeable. I make a mental note to talk to him about controlling his body language. "What do you think we're missing out on?"

Ever the try-hard, Caden suggests, "More news content?"

"No." Frank releases him. "Leave that to CNN." He balls his fists together and raises them to his shoulders. "We're missing personability." He walks to the front of the room and grips the table. "Who here has put their real life into their work?"

No one raises their hand—and for good reason. We all keep work separate from our personal lives. I may give advice and live up to The Modern Gentleman persona, but I don't ever tell my readers about my specific experiences. I'm not a personal anecdote-giving guy. I try to keep things as basic as possible, as separate as possible.

"Exactly!" Frank jabs his finger into the air. "We're missing a huge opportunity. Who are the career-driven people working at HYPE? What do they do when they part ways with their computers at the end of the day? What are their hobbies? What are their interests? Do they take cooking classes?"

Roman mumbles, "Does Love Swipe count as a hobby?"

From the corner of my eye, I see Caden elbow Roman, who chuckles to himself.

With too much passion in his movements, Frank starts moving around the room again, hand back to hovering over employees' heads. "We need to humanize this company, connect with our public, show them they aren't alone in this crazy, unpredictable world."

I sit back and listen to Frank ramble on about his new idea, relieved I only write an advice column. Based on Frank's enthusiasm, I can see the painful journey some of my colleagues will have to endure.

"That brings me to your new assignments. It's time to get personal . . . personal," Frank singsongs an off-key version of "Let's Get Physical." This man, Jesus. It's as if the eccentricities of

Johnny Depp had a baby with the trying-too-hard Michael Scott. He's a vision, that's for damn sure.

Making his way around the room, he hovers over Darla and places his hand on her shoulder. Her face says it all—an *oh hell* crossing her features. "Darla, your recipe videos have been informational, but I want more. For the next month, you will take subscribers into your kitchen and show them the ins and outs of your nightly ritual in front of the stove. I'm thinking apron, paper grocery bag on the counter, and that bright smile of yours." Christ, that's invasive. She nods and starts taking notes. Poor Darla.

I stretch my legs out and lean back in my chair, trying to predict who he's going to target next.

"Keith . . ." *Oh shit.* He runs the adult content. "The erogenous zones of a man. What are they? What makes them tickle? How can you get them humming? This month I want you to experiment with your body and different techniques for how to get the male anatomy up and running." Oh fuck, I hold back a chuckle as Keith turns white. "Charmaine, I want you to work on the same article but from the female point of view. Focus on your arousal and don't be generic. Really dig deep."

"Dig deep," Roman mumbles and laughs like the hung-over, immature asshole he is.

Frank divvies out three more assignments. There's a piece on family tree genetic testing, which didn't seem too terrible until Frank required pictures of all family members for visual references. He assigned a pregnancy article to the only pregnant woman in the office, Sunny, who luckily pulled her HR card when he mentioned doctor visits. Good for her. And then there's the battle with adult acne. Oh Greg, hang in there, man.

I grip the table, ready for this shindig to end, while Frank goes into detail with Greg about all the angles he can focus on. Slow-motion charcoal mask videos being a "high ticket" piece. I look at my watch and realize we've been in this meeting for over an hour now. If we can move past blackheads, that would be appreciated.

"I'm going to die if we don't get out of here soon," Roman

mutters to me. "I need water, man, or a cheeseburger, something, because my stomach is churning. I don't think I've ever been this close to death."

I lean toward him and say quietly, "Don't drink so much next time, and you won't have that problem."

"I told you, Crazy Town, okay? She was drinking her weight in vodka. I had to keep up."

"You really didn't. You could have—"

"And that brings us to our final participant, Wes."

Er . . . say what?

I look behind me and standing plain as day with a gigantic grin on his face is Frank. In slow motion, I watch his hand move from the collar of his purple jacket to my shoulder. I want to melt into my chair, disappear, anything to avoid that touch, the touch that could alter my entire career trajectory.

"This is the assignment I'm most excited about. It's more of an experiment actually."

Experiment? Oh hell. The thought of quitting passes through my mind for a second before I scratch that idea. Being unemployed isn't going to pay the rent for my apartment overlooking Central Park West. And no job is going to pay me as well as Frank does, that's for damn sure.

"We all know the popularity The Modern Gentleman has brought to HYPE, but I think it's time we take it up a notch." From the corner of my eye, I see Roman hanging his head over the table, chuckling to himself. Such an asshole. "Your advice is great, but I want to see it in action. Your new assignment, Wes, is to no longer be single."

Dread fills me. No longer *be* single? It's not like it's by my choosing. I haven't found the right girl yet. "I love reading your column but if you think about it, there's no validity behind it. You're a single man handing out dating advice from behind a persona you've created. I think it's time The Modern Gentleman put his advice to the test."

I am so not liking where this is heading.

"You are to take us through the process, the steps of securing a relationship the way The Modern Gentleman would. Show us it can be done, that in today's society of digital media, online relationships, and a world of divorce, you can still manage to find love through a modernized version of chivalry." He squeezes my shoulder tightly. "I'm so excited."

He turns to address the rest of the room. "Think *How to Lose a Guy in Ten Days*, but the opposite. Show readers, these modern gentlemen, the proper way to court. I will need articles at the end of each week with your status update. We're rolling out these pieces in a month, so get cracking. Meet with your directors for weekly progress reports and let them know if you have questions. You're dismissed."

Take us through the process.

As if it's that easy—to go out and start dating someone, let alone date someone for work.

With my tablet in hand and an annoying weight on my shoulders, I go to stand when Frank catches my eye. "I'm extremely excited about your assignment, Wes. You can revamp the image given to today's man. It isn't about beer, boners, and Buffalo wings anymore. It's about a proper shave, the right sports jacket, and the way you seduce a woman in the bedroom."

I can't hide the cringe this time. "Frank, with all due respect, don't you think that's bordering on too personal? Talking about my sex life?"

"Not at all. That's the point. Real-life experiences. It's what people are drawn to. You can spout off all the advice you want, but unless you're actually in the thick of it, your opinion is moot. It's time to prove you deserve your title as The Modern Gentleman." He slaps my back. "Go get 'em. I'm giving you a week to find the right woman to pursue—and if you can't within a week, I'll step in and help." He pauses and rebuttons his jacket, which he opened during his *exhilarating* meeting. "Don't let it get to that point."

Without another word, he retreats the conference room, leaving Roman and Caden laughing behind me.

"Dude, have fun with that," Roman quickly says before holding his stomach and stalking off toward his office.

Still in shock, I turn to Caden, who shrugs. "Not going to lie, your life just took a turn toward the shitter."

I couldn't agree more. How could this not be a nightmare assignment?

CHAPTER THREE

Dear Modern Gentleman,
    I think I might have messed up last night. I mean, totally fucked up my image in front of the girl I've been dying to take out for months. I wound up working late with her, and, trying to be a gentleman, asked if I could walk her to her car. I kept telling myself, think about The Modern Gentleman and what he would do. I think I was too caught up in my anxiety because when we got to her car, I, uh, I told her she "looked swell." I've never used that word before in my entire life, and I don't think anyone has in the last couple of decades. I could tell by the way she scrunched her nose and thanked me politely that she thought it was weird. Then she retreated into her car and drove away before I could say anything to redeem myself. I don't know if there is any recovering this. Help, please!
    The Swell Guy

Dear Swell Guy,
    Man, that's rough. When I say to embrace the gentleman in you, I don't mean the gentleman from the nineteen twenties. But don't worry; this is totally repairable. The good news: you complimented her, in a weird way, yes, but you complimented her. So move forward with that. Try complimenting her every day, but this time, with some more hip lingo. Try

rad—that's a few decades closer. *Smirks* All in all, Gent, you're on the right track, so keep at it. I'm sure it will be something you can laugh about later.

Good luck, Gent.

The Modern Gentleman

WES

The Prowl

"Got you all signed up." Roman plops down on the barstool next to me. "Your username is CockDaddy69 and I used your picture from the staff directory. Go ahead, start swiping." He holds out his phone, which I don't bother taking.

"I'm not going to use Love Swipe—how many times do I have to tell you that? And I'm sure as hell not using it under the name CockDaddy69."

"Wes, you have three more days before Frank steps in. You've been out every night for the past four nights and have yet to approach anyone. You're toeing the line of desperation."

"He's right." Caden sips from his tumbler. "Your chances of finding someone now aren't looking promising. You might want to start swiping."

"I'm not swiping. Jesus." I sip my whiskey and suck in my cheeks when the heat of the drink hits my taste buds. "We're talking about The Modern Gentleman here. There is no way he would start a relationship on Love Swipe."

"What about Bumble?" Roman asks. "That's more for good girls, and they get to make the first move."

"I'm not using a dating app."

"Why not? It's the modern way to date. You have access to

thousands of potential dates at your fingertips. Why wouldn't you want to utilize that?" Roman asks, clearly insulted I'm putting down his method. "I know plenty of people who've met the love of their life on dating sites."

"My sister did," Caden adds. "They're going on five years now."

I sigh and lean against the bar as I face the crowd of people. "I'm not knocking dating sites, especially when they're used the correct way. They're great actually, especially for people like your sister, who are on the shy side, or like your brother-in-law, who couldn't find someone to connect with on an intellectual level. That's not the problem."

"Then what is?" Roman asks, exasperated.

"It's just not how I envisioned meeting someone. I might be living the modern side of life, but I want to meet someone the old-fashioned way."

Caden leans forward and taps Roman on the knee. "He wants a meet-cute."

Roman nods and with a smarmy smile, he adds, "He's such a romantic little teddy bear, isn't he?"

"Don't be dicks. Is it too much to ask to have a story to tell my grandchildren one day? A story that will blow them away? I don't want to tell them I swiped right and the rest was history."

Roman sips his drink and leans back against the bar. "Sounds romantic to me." Turning serious, he asks, "Why do you think this person you're supposed to meet is going to be *the one*? This is only for an assignment at work, man, not the woman you're going to marry."

"He's right." Caden's phone rings. He checks it and gets up from his stool. "It's work, got to take this." Turning to me, he says, "Just pick someone, it only has to last a month. After that, you can meet the love of your life any way you want."

When Caden takes off, phone attached to his ear, Roman tries to hand me his phone again. "Come on, CockDaddy69, take a look."

I shake my head. "And what, tell my readers I used Love Swipe? Come on, that goes against everything I've been preaching."

"They're not going to know the difference. Just find a damn woman and conjure up your own meet-cute in your head." He holds the phone out to me. "Look, there are women less than a mile away from here who you can meet up with. There might even be some in this bar right now."

I bite the inside of my cheek, trying to decide what to do. I really don't want Frank to get involved. Something tells me I'd end up with Francine, his daughter, and the female version of him. I shudder inwardly and take Roman's phone. Desperation is knocking.

And besides, I can come up with a meet-cute. I'm a writer and I've watched enough romantic comedies to make something up for the column—anything to avoid Frank's choice.

"That a boy. Now look through the pics and see if there is anyone . . . oh, look at her tits. Pick her."

Of course that would be the first thing Roman notices. Although, she does have nice boobs, but . . .

"She likes the Red Sox." Deal-breaker, I don't care how nice her boobs are or how desperate I am.

"Oh fuck that shit. Go back to Boston," Roman yells at the phone. "Your tits aren't that great." Yankees fans to the core—can you tell?

As I look through the women Love Swipe suggests, I feel like a total asshole swiping left on their profiles. That's what's so wrong about this way of doing things—it's all based on the first glance. What if the girl isn't good at taking selfies, or maybe she thinks duck lips are attractive? She could actually have a beautiful soul and I'd never know.

"This is fucked up, man," I say as Roman takes over, swiping left at a consistent pace, not giving any woman *not to his ideal* a second thought.

"You have to be cutthroat, man." His swiping picks up speed.

"Left, left, left. You're not into blondes or women who wear turtle-necks. Or women who are left-handed. Left, left, left."

"I have nothing against turtlenecks or left-handed women," I admonish.

"I sure as hell do. Turtlenecks were designed by the devil himself and damn if I will have two different can openers in my apartment because I'm with a left-handed woman." Roman continues to swipe as I look out at the crowd, trying to ignore his idiocy while surveying the people around us. Most of the bar-goers are single—you can tell from the way they stand together in their comfortable pods. The sexes are mostly divided, men eyeing their prey, and women giving them a show.

From the outside looking in, it's actually an interesting thing to observe. The way men—

"Dude, this girl right here." Roman nudges me and puts his phone in front of my face. "Look at her. She's perfect. Innocent-looking, has a sweet face. There's no way she'll take you to Freakville."

I grab his phone and take in the girl Roman found. Brown hair, brown eyes, a sweet smile . . . huh, she actually seems like a normal, all-American girl.

"Swipe right, man, and start a conversation." Sighing and hating every second of this, I swipe right, hoping to God she hasn't swiped left on me. I blame Frank for this. "Look, it's a match." Roman shakes me as the screen lights up. "She must be prowling as we speak. Send her a message"

Shit, she swiped right on CockDaddy69.

Did I mention I hate this? Trying to make the most of this situation, I type out a greeting.

Cockdaddy69: *Hi*

"Hi? That's all you're going to say? That's entirely too lame. Someone with the username Cockdaddy69 would not just say hi."

"You're the idiot who picked out the name, not me. What do you want me to say?"

"Maybe something like, 'I like your pictures.'"

"That's pervert level. Everything about this makes me feel like a pervert." Roman's phone dings in my hand.

BrowniesYum: *Hi, CockDaddy69. I'm glad you messaged me. You wouldn't happen to be at the Bowery Bar right now? I just saw this really cute guy and tried to find him on Love Swipe. I think you might be him.*

"She's in the bar."

"She is?" Roman sticks his head up over the crowd and starts looking around. "I don't see her."

"Sit the fuck down." I yank on his shirt and force him back onto his stool. "Can you try to make this less humiliating?"

"Stop putzing around and make a move. Come on, dude, it's either this lady or Frank's daughter."

I run my hand over my face, already exhausted, and message her back.

Cockdaddy69: *Come say hi in person. I want to get to know you.*

"Oh, smooth, I like it." Roman takes his phone back and pockets it. He throws his drink back and tosses some cash on the bar. "I'm going to head out, I'm meeting up with Crazy Town again tonight."

I shake my head. "The toe sucker? Didn't you learn your lesson the other night?"

He cringes from the whiskey he just downed and sets the empty tumbler on the bar. "What can I say? She intrigues me. See you in the morning. I expect a full report."

Roman takes off, leaving me alone. I lean against the bar casually, swirling my drink. *Crap.* What if BrowniesYum is talking about another guy? Maybe she meant Roman . . . and he's already left. *Shit.* Just as I'm about to ditch this experiment altogether, I feel a tap on my shoulder and turn to find BrowniesYum, holding a tall, fruity drink. She's even more gorgeous in person. Long tanned legs, slim hips, a decent-sized chest, and a very beautiful face. Her hair falls past her shoulders in waves and her lips are painted bright red. Thank you, Love Swipe.

Standing from my stool, I greet her with a smile. "BrowniesYum?"

"Yup, that's me."

She smiles, cups my neck, and pulls me in for a brief hug. Damn, she smells good too. Maybe Roman has the right idea, after all. As she pulls away, her hair brushes against me and I catch a whiff of lavender. Nice touch.

"It's nice to meet you."

I offer her a seat, and when she's situated, she takes a sip of her drink, eyeing me over the rim. "It's nice to meet you too." She looks around. "Where did your friend go?"

"He had plans to meet up with someone."

"So that means it's just us?"

And a bar full of hungry singles, but I won't mention that.

"Just us. I'm Wes, by the way." I stick out my hand, which she shakes. Her hand is so small and petite . . . and soft. Brownies Yum is not a bad catch at all.

"It's nice to meet you, Wes. I'm Lois."

And all the hype behind this woman immediately deflates.

Lois . . .

Nope.

Nope, nope, nope. I quickly pull my hand away from her grasp. This isn't going to work.

This is why you should never meet people on apps where they have usernames, because you end up in a situation like this. A situation where the girl you're interested in has the same exact name as your own damn mother.

In no possible way will this work. I can't speak for the entire male population, but come on. No man in his right mind would want to date a girl with the same name as his mom. It doesn't matter how hot she is, because when it comes down to it, the last thing you want to be saying while your dick is hard is your mom's name.

Give it to me, Lois.

Squeeze me, Lois.

Ride me . . . Lois.

Oh fuck, nope.

Not going to happen.

Lois . . . I would rather call her Brownies Yum.

"Are you okay?" She presses her hand on my arm, a concerned look on her face, but instead of seeing Brownies Yum and her gorgeous face, all I can see is my mother. My mother in her large purple glasses and her Winnie the Pooh shirt.

Talk about a mood killer.

Not wanting to act like a dickhead, I clear my throat. "Yeah. Sorry about that." I straighten up and act like the gentleman I try to portray. "What do you do . . . *Lois?*"

She runs her hand invitingly up my chest. "I do men like you."

Yeahhhhh, I can't do this. Normally I'd have absolutely no problem with a woman running her fingers up my chest, but I can't stop thinking about that Winnie the Pooh shirt and if I don't break this off right now, I'm pretty sure my penis will never unbury itself from my scrotum.

The moment I slide off my barstool and step away, her face falls. I feel a twinge of guilt. This isn't her fault. Given different circumstances I'd be happy to continue the conversation, but ending the night with Lois is *not* something I want to experience.

Knowing I need to be honest, I square up, like the man I taught myself to be. "Lois, I have to be straight with you. You're gorgeous, and normally I'd be asking for your number by now, but unfortunately, you have the same name as my mom and it's just weird for me."

She scrunches her nose. "Your mom's name is Lois?"

I nod apologetically. "Yeah, it's an inconvenient coincidence."

She quirks her mouth to the side, a pinch in her brow. "And you can't get over that?"

Is she insane? Of course I can't get over that. Making out with a woman named Lois surprisingly isn't on a list of things I'd like to partake in.

I chuckle. "Would you be able to get over it if I had the same name as your dad?"

She smirks at that and reaches out to play with one of the

buttons on my shirt. "Wouldn't faze me since I'd call you daddy anyway."

Did you see that? That right there, that was her freak flag waving high and proud. Should have known swiping right was a bad idea.

I take a step back. "Lois, it was a pleasure meeting you, but I think I'm going to head out."

I leave money on the bar, give her a sorry smile, and head toward the bar exit. Sorry, BrowniesYum, it isn't going to happen for us.

Standing on the curb, I wave down a taxi and pull out my phone. After I give the cab driver my address, I call Roman. He picks up after two rings.

"Please tell me all the swiping paid off and you're about to land this girl."

"I left."

He sighs into the phone. "Dude, what the hell is—"

"Her name was Lois."

There's silence on the other line and then Roman says, "Lois, as in your mom's name?"

"Yeah." Since traffic isn't heavy, we cruise uptown through the streets of New York City, lights flashing by, dew glistening off the sidewalks, and the city's night owls still prowling the streets.

"Man, that's bad luck, but I still would have done her."

I shake my head. "You would have had sex with someone who has the same name as your mom?"

"No way in hell, but I've always wanted to bang Winnie the Pooh right off your mom's shirt so I'd have gone for it."

"Fuck you, man." I laugh.

Laughing himself, he asks, "Want me to swipe for you again?"

"No. Cockdaddy69 is retired. Looks like I'm going to have to do this the old-fashioned way."

The way I prefer—through coincidence, conversation, and confidence.

CHAPTER FOUR

D ear Modern Gentleman,
      The dating pool is a bitch. A few months ago, I broke up with my girlfriend of three years and now my friends are begging me to get back into the dating circuit. Being three years out has made me rusty and self-conscious—everything has changed. There are rules and apps and protocols, and I can't keep up with any of it. So I decided to jump in headfirst and join Love Swipe. I met a girl I thought was super chill. We went out for drinks and dancing. Had an awesome time. I asked about a second date and she said yes, except, she wants to have a threesome with her gay best friend. I really like this girl, but I'm not sure about a threesome. What do you think?

Sincerely,
Rusty and Nervous

Dear Rusty and Nervous,
      First of all, congratulations on putting yourself back out into the dating world. It's a scary place to be, but once you find the right woman, it's going to be worth it. Second of all, your first mistake was looking for someone on Love Swipe. That particular app doesn't always encourage the most gentlemanly behavior. My advice to you: be a gentleman and politely say

you're not interested. When the time comes to get intimate, I'd let her know that you fuck her and her alone. Modern Gentlemen don't share their women.

Good luck, Gent,
The Modern Gentleman

WES

THE MEET-CUTE

"Wishing Lois was still in the picture?" Roman asks as he shoots a three-pointer and makes it with ease.

It's Sunday, and the courts are crowded once again on this warm, sunny morning in Central Park. Pickup games surround us as testosterone floats through the air. And even though Sundays on the court are my favorite part of the week, I can't help but feel uneasy, slightly frustrated, and a lot like I'm about to throw up.

Why, you ask? Probably because I've yet to meet someone, and I have to report to Frank tomorrow morning. Not going to lie, I wish Lois *was* still in the picture. That's how desperate I am.

Sighing, I answer Roman. "Would it be sick of me to say yes?"

"It would," Caden answers, dribbling the ball and shooting from where Roman sunk his shot. "It's a common rule in every man's rulebook: don't date a woman who has the same name as your mother."

Caden sinks his shot as well. I'm an S and an E away from losing at Horse. I normally dominate, but my head is spinning with my dilemma, and I haven't been able to concentrate or shoot worth shit.

"I'm fucked," I say as I shoot and miss terribly.

"Frank is going to set you up with his daughter—you know that, right?" Roman asks.

The thought has crossed my mind many times. Francine has already expressed interest in me, not being shy about it at all with her blatant flirting and wildly inappropriate touching. The only reason I haven't reported her ass-grabbing to HR is my fear of getting fired by Frank. So, she squeezes my tush whenever she gets a chance. Nepotism at its finest right there.

"I know," I sigh and grab the back of my head as Roman makes another three-pointer, this time along the baseline of the court. "I need to avoid her at all costs."

Caden misses, which gives me control to shoot the ball from wherever I want. I choose my sweet spot in the top right corner of the three-point line and sink it. "What about your sister, Roman? Think Carmen would want to do me a favor?"

"Not Carmen," Caden says quickly, drawing our attention. He looks between us and stretches his arms behind his back, striking a casual pose that fools no one. "What? It's a rule: don't fuck with each other's sisters. Bro code, man."

"It's a favor," I point out. "It's not fucking around with her."

"Sure as hell isn't fucking around with her," Roman cuts in. "She just moved here. I don't need you two idiots messing with her. The city is scary enough as it is."

"I'll pay her," I say out of pure desperation.

"No. Christ, man. Have some self-respect."

He's right, I have zero right now.

"You know, I'm genuinely surprised," Caden says as he dribbles the ball. "Out of all the guys in the office, I'd have assumed you'd be the one who could easily pick someone up, given your status and all." He wiggles his eyebrows at me.

"Picking someone up is completely different than pursuing and dating someone. The two don't go hand in hand. Picking someone up is a one-time deal, and you don't necessarily have to have a conversation. You're cordial, you fuck, and then you bid your adieus. When you're looking to date someone, there has to be a connection there—it can't all be about tits and ass."

"It's always about tits and ass," Roman answers, sinking another ball.

"Is that what you're teaching Carmen?" I joke as Caden misses.

"Hell no. Carmen knows one thing and one thing only: how secure her chastity belt is."

I chuckle as I catch the ball on a bounce from Caden. "So sexist, man." I take a look at the hoop, firmly plant my feet, and shoot. I miss. Shit, my game is way off today. Not bothering to stick around to see who wins, I say, "I'm out. I have some searching to do."

"Good luck with that," Roman calls out. "I'm hoping you don't meet anyone, because I'm dying to see you with Francine."

A gentleman would hold back his response and wouldn't let his friend egg him on. But right now, I'm not feeling very gentlemanly so I flip him my middle finger as I walk away. Their laughter rings through the fenced-in basketball court, irritating the hell out of me.

Phone in hand, I walk across Central Park, dodging tourists and kids chasing each other through the vast green space in the heart of New York City. Couples hold hands as they pass by, laughing and enjoying each other's company, sending a not-so-subtle reminder that I'm in the clusterfuck of my life.

Shit.

When I started The Modern Gentleman, I never believed it would dive into my personal life, but then again, Frank is a wild card. I should have known that from the day I first met him.

I was a year out of a three-year relationship and still recovering. She broke up with me. How could that be, right? Well, surprise, I wasn't always the pristine, well-mannered, fuck-sation you see today. I was one of them: a beer-guzzling, video-game-playing, disinterested asshole who took my relationship for granted. I spent more time charming my buds in bars than paying attention to my girl's needs. And one day, she'd had enough.

She dumped me and dumped me fucking hard, broke my heart, and found a man who treated her with all the respect she deserved. It took me a few months to get my ass in gear, but once I did, I focused on becoming the epitome of what every man in this damn city should aspire to be. I cultivated my gentlemanly behavior in public and my alpha tendencies in the bedroom. I lived the life, created a persona, and sold it within minutes of interviewing with Frank at HYPE.

Do I hate being The Modern Gentleman day in and day out? Sometimes. And the pressure to live up to my own rules can be palpable, especially right fucking now.

There has to be someone I can contact, someone who has a friend of a friend who is available, right? I mentally scroll through my phone's contacts list.

Of course Roman and Caden were no help. Carmen could have been a really good option but Roman was definitely not on board with that idea. If I was a lesser man, I'd call her out of spite, but I do have standards and respecting friends' boundaries is one of them.

Annoyed, I pull on my hair and look down at my phone, considering going on another dating app, despite—

"STOP," a woman screams, halting me in my place.

Frozen and slightly terrified, I look around for whoever yelled at me, just as a flash of red swoops by at my feet. Startled, I step back to find a petite woman with deep red, wavy hair on all fours. A plastic baggie covers her hand as she scoops something up from the walkway.

What the hell?

Before I can ask what she's doing, she pops up from the ground and turns the bag inside out. Facing me, she holds it out and says, "Take this."

Caught off guard, I take the bag, which smells like a dead carcass, and hold it out in front of me, trying to waft the smell in the other direction.

Glancing down, I realize that in fact, yes, I'm holding a sack of dog crap.

Right there, all gross and warm, dangling from my hand, is poop.

This is a first.

The redhead squats next to a dog, offering up a bowl of water. "Drink up, little one, you don't want to get dehydrated," she coos at a tiny beagle, who's sporting one ear and gray hair on his snout.

Unsure what to do and feeling like I'm barging in on an intimate moment, I clear my throat and ask, "Uh, would you like me to tie this up and throw it away for you?"

She gives me a once-over and sneers. Literally, sneers. Her nose curls up and a look of abhorrence hits me square in the chest. *You disgust me*, her eyes speak scornfully.

Not the most pleasant of greetings. "Serves you right, you know," she snaps.

"Serves me right? What's that supposed to mean?"

She pats the beagle on the head and stands, dusting off her gray workout capris. It's the first time I get a good look at her and damn, is it weird to say I'd hold her dog poop any time?

She's gorgeous. Her vibrant, dark red hair frames a heart-shaped face that's free of makeup. The freckles kissing her nose give her an air of innocence, but the upturn in her turquoise eyes makes her look sexy as hell.

When she crosses her arms over her chest, taking a defensive pose, I can't help but notice her ample cleavage in a teal tank top and black sports bra.

"I should have let you step in the dog poop," she declares with hostility.

Well, that's fucking rude.

Interested to find out what her aversion to me is, I ask, "And why is that?"

She points to the phone in my hand, the hand that's not holding the sack of dog poop out in front of me. "Operating a mobile device while walking should be illegal. Today it could have been dog poop, tomorrow it could be a baby that fell out of his stroller."

Okay . . .

"If a baby falls out of his stroller, that's on the parent, not me."

"Not if you were aware of your surroundings. A gentleman wouldn't have his head buried in his phone, but rather he would be prepared to react to any situation around him. If you were aware, with your head up, the baby wouldn't have never fallen out of his stroller because you would have caught him."

A gentleman? She's giving me lessons on how to be a gentleman? Little does she know who she's talking to.

Although . . .

She's right. One of the things I preach is being cognizant of your surroundings and to anticipate every situation around you. Damn. She's schooling me in my best subject.

Feeling defensive, I ask, "So you're telling me you never operate a mobile phone while walking."

"Don't need to. I don't have one." The smug look on her face should annoy me, but for some odd reason, it makes me smile.

"You're telling me in an age of having the world at our fingertips, you don't have a cell phone?"

"The only phone I carry around is a prepaid flip phone I use for emergencies and calls with my agent."

Agent, interesting. Assessing her one more time, I take in her appearance, her posture, and the confidence she exudes.

"Actress?" I ask.

"Yes, musical theater."

I arch an eyebrow. "Really? Broadway?"

Her eyes turn dreamy as she presses her palms together and looks up to the sky. "One day, hopefully."

Ah, an aspiring Broadway actress. Tough business, but there's something about this woman that makes me think she'll get to Broadway. Besides, she's yet to take the poop bag from me, which takes a lot of I-don't-give-a-fuck attitude, an attitude necessary to survive in that world.

"That's an admirable aspiration. With a lot of hard work and big dreams, you'll get there." Cheesy as it may sound, I mean every word. I encourage anyone to reach for what they want in life. Life isn't worth living if you're not living it for what you want.

There is a quirk to her lip when she takes in my words. She eyes the poop bag and takes it from me, her fingers brushing against mine briefly and sending a small tingle down my spine. She twists the top of the bag and ties it off in one smooth motion. With a flick of her wrist, barely looking, she tosses the bag into the trash can a few feet away, scoring two poop points.

Damn.

"You're not so bad." She assesses me. "Besides being one of those people who can't seem to take their eyes off their phone to experience the world in front of them, you seem pretty cool."

"Yeah?" I stick my hands in my shorts pockets and rock back on my heels. "And why's that?"

"I've been in this business long enough to notice the disbelief in peoples' faces when I tell them what I'm trying to do. You didn't give it to me. You actually seemed impressed."

"I am." I shrug. "It's not every day you almost step on the feces that belong to a dog with a missing ear whose owner is an aspiring Broadway actress. Almost seems like I hit the jackpot." I wink.

She points her finger at me knowingly. "Ah, a charmer. I should have guessed. What man wears workout clothes but still has impeccable hair?"

I smirk inwardly. A who has a certain persona to keep up.

"Never know who you're going to run into on a Sunday in the park." I nod at her dog. "What's your dog's name?"

"General Fitzbum, but he's not my dog. I'm a dog walker, one of my many jobs." She's not the least bit ashamed of having multiple jobs, unlike some other people I've met. She almost says it with pride. I like that about her.

"General Fitzbum? Interesting name." I squat down and scratch him behind his ear. "What happened to his other ear?"

"I was told he was born like that. Mrs. Fitzbum is an author who spends most of her days locked up in her office, so she hired me to offer some fresh air to the general. She thinks he was born with only one ear because he's her grandfather reincarnated, and her grandfather lost his ear in World War I. Because of that, she wanted to give him an honorable name." She pauses. "An odd lady, that one. Only drinks orange soda. Says it helps her write."

I pat the general a few more times and then stand. "Whatever helps, right?" Extending my hand, I say, "I'm Wes, by the way."

"Wes. It's lovely to meet you. I'm June. June Lacy."

"June," I say, liking how her name rolls off my tongue easily. "Pretty name."

"Thanks." She looks at her watch and cringes. "I should be going. It was nice talking to you. Remember to look up, enjoy the world around you, Wes. Breathe it all in. You will always have time to look at your phone. But the world is a fascinating place, so soak it up." With a wink, she takes off with the general.

Panic sets in.

I don't want her to leave. Not yet. I was just warming up. I want to get to know her better, I want to hear more about the general, about her multiple jobs, about her aspirations. She can't leave.

Not when she's the perfect prospect for my dating project.

What better way to start an article than "We met over dog feces"?

I need to ask her out.

Now.

Fumbling over my words, unable to speak and in a state of sheer panic, I jog after her, only to trip over a crack in the pavement and stumble forward, knocking into her from behind.

So fucking graceful.

We both waver between almost eating pavement and catching our balance. Once steadied, she turns to give me a *what the hell are you doing* look.

She might be nice, but this girl's sneers.

Holy hell.

For the first time I can remember, I'm speechless, completely out of my element, with absolutely no control over what happens next . . .

"Food with me!" I blurt out like a robot, sounding like a complete jackass. I promise, I'm so much smoother than this, but with my deadline approaching, my looming desperation, and actually liking this girl, I've lost any semblance of cool. Clearing my throat, and trying to straighten myself, I say, "I mean, would you like to have dinner with me?"

Not as smooth as I'd like, but it works.

"Dinner?" June asks with a raised eyebrow. "Have dinner with a man who almost stepped in dog poop today because he was too engrossed in his phone?"

I swallow hard, knowing she makes a fair point. "I'd be honored if you gave me a chance."

She eyes me again, biting the side of her lip, uncertainty in her eyes. "Dinner seems like a risk. I don't think I can commit to over an hour with you just yet."

Er . . . what? Maybe her hesitation is coming from the way I asked her out. I did shout at her. If it was a text, it would have been all caps, except, she wouldn't have gotten the text since she has a prepaid phone. Christ.

She looks down at her watch again, before studying me. "I have to take the general out at five thirty tomorrow night. I prefer the protection of a one-eared dog in case you turn out to be a real creep. At least I know the general will have my six. Care to join me for a walk tomorrow?"

Bartering.

Date bartering. That's what my life has become.

"How about a picnic?" I counter, stepping closer, raising the stakes, feeling more like myself, now that she's giving me a smidgen of hope. "The general seems to think I'm good people." I kneel down and scratch behind his ear again. He leans into my hand. "See, he approves."

"He's leading you on." She pushes her sultry hair behind her shoulder and says, "It's a walk or it's nothing. Take it or leave it, Mr. Fancy Hair."

Conceding and not wanting to push her anymore, I stand. "I'll take it."

"Smart choice." She pats my shoulder. "See you tomorrow."

When she turns to walk away again, I have to stop her. "Wait, how will I get in touch with you? You don't have a cell phone. Do you have a landline?"

"I do."

"Can I have your number then?"

She shakes her head. "You have to earn that number, Wes."

Hell.

"Then how do I know where to meet you tomorrow?"

She motions to the open, tree-lined walkway. An elderly couple sits on the nearest bench, feeding the pigeons birdseed beneath a wonky-looking tree. "Let's just refer to this as our magical spot, our meet-cute, the Wes-and-June headquarters. Meet me here at five thirty tomorrow and don't forget . . ." She reaches out and tilts my chin up. "Eyes up, Wes." With a slight smile, she drops my chin and turns. As she's walking away, her beautiful hair swishing across her back, she calls over her shoulder, "See you tomorrow, Mr. Fancy Hair."

For a few moments, I watch her walk away, her pert ass swaying with each step and her lithe body gathering all my attention. I run my fingers through my "fancy" hair, stunned by what just happened.

First of all, I need to work on my goddamn charm because it was seriously lacking just now. There was no modern gentleman in sight, just an awkward man in workout clothes who almost stepped in poop. I sigh. Not the best material for an article.

Second, this woman is different. Confident, aloof, knows what she wants, and is interesting as hell, with a touch of quirk. There is a mystery about her, something guarded that I could see in her eyes. I'm intrigued. I want to see who this woman is—this woman who doesn't believe in cell phones, who walks a one-eared dog for a living, and who has an addictive spark in her eye when you mention the theater.

And third, Roman and Caden can kiss my ass. Their hopes and dreams of watching me trying to date Frank's daughter have been squashed. Francine is a distant memory.

Now it's all about June.

CHAPTER FIVE

D*ear Modern Gentleman,*
    I would love to get your take on mixing scents. Between after-shave, hair products, deodorant, and cologne, I feel like one giant fragrance store walking around the streets of New York City. I swear someone tried to give me twenty dollars the other day for a glimpse inside my jacket to see what I was selling. Teach me your ways of the scents.
    Smells Too Good

Dear Smells Too Good,
Let's start by saying, at least you don't smell like the rat you see scampering around on the subway tracks with a bag of Fritos hanging out of his mouth. Give yourself credit for that. As for all the scents you have going on, skip the aftershave, not necessary with cologne. And it might take some time and a lot of sniffing, but try to find scents that complement each other. I, myself, go for a fresh, woodsy scent in everything I choose. Be the guy who brings his deodorant and hair product to the cologne counter. Have no shame, sniff it up, and keep smelling good.
Good luck, Gent,
The Modern Gentleman

WES

THE THREAT

When I walk through the doors of HYPE on this beautiful Monday morning, I can't help but have a little pep in my step, a little bounce in my loafers, a little cock to my swagger. (Cock as in cockiness, not as in dick—just wanted to clarify.) My weekend was plagued by horrendous thoughts of how this morning would pan out. All I could envision was Frank pulling me into his office, where he would give me the go-ahead to pursue his daughter. Just the thought of that conversation had my penis starting to turn itself inside out.

But now . . .

Fuck, I'm high-fiving people this morning, which for the record, I never do. High-fiving is for jocks and frat boys, not gentlemen. But hell if I can stop myself. June swooped in with the general and saved the day.

After my morning routine, I arrive at my office door to find Caden and Roman waiting, their arms crossed over their chests and smart-ass smiles on their faces. I stopped myself from texting them about June last night so I could see their expressions in person when I told them the news. The best part about all of this will be wiping the smirks off their smug faces.

"Roman, surprised to see you alert this early in the morning." I push past both of them and into my office. They follow closely behind.

"I went to bed early, drank some electrolytes for breakfast, and practically ran to the office this morning." He rubs his hands together. "I couldn't miss your big day." The dickhead is practically frothing at the mouth in excitement. No wonder he didn't want me to ask his sister to help me—he wanted to revel in my misery.

Sounds about right. He's a good friend, but when he can witness my balls getting busted, he always takes a front-row seat.

Caden leans against the doorframe to my office, arms still crossed. "Have you prepared yourself? Do you know what you're going to say to Frank if he suggests Francine?"

I pick up a pile of letters from my desk and stack them together. "Not worried about it."

Roman jabs his thumb at me while he talks to Caden. "Denial. He wore his denial pants today. They're cute, but reality will knock him in the dick soon."

"Reality knocked me in the dick yesterday," I reply.

Both Roman and Caden converge on me. Roman leans over my desk and asks, "Did Francine already get her claws in you?"

"Nope." I smile at both of them. "Met a girl yesterday."

"No, you fucking didn't," Roman counters.

"I did."

Margaret, Frank's secretary, sticks her head into my office with a light knock. "Sorry to interrupt your conversation, but Frank would like to see you, Wes."

"Thank you, Margaret. I'll be right there."

I button my suit jacket and head toward the door of my office when Caden stops me with a hand to my chest. "Did you really meet someone?"

I pull on the sleeves of my button-up shirt and smile at my friend. "I did."

"Bullshit." Roman steps in. "What's her name?" He eyes me suspiciously.

Without skipping a beat, I answer, "June Lacy. She's a stage actress, and we're meeting up today at five thirty. Sorry to burst your bubble, boys, but since you seemed so interested in Francine, Roman, I'll be sure to put in a good word with Frank. Maybe he'll be happy to see you date his daughter."

"Mention my name in that office and I'll slice your balls off."

I chuckle. "I'm more of a man than to throw you under the bus like that. I'm a gentleman, for fuck's sake."

As I walk toward Frank's office, Caden calls out, "Pretty sure gentlemen don't say 'for fuck's sake.'"

They don't, but I can afford a slip-up every once in a while.

Frank's face lights up when I walk into his office. "There he is, the man I'm excited to talk to. Take a seat, take a seat." He's bouncing in his chair. His hair's slicked back today instead of a coiffed wave on the top of his head. He's the only man I know who has a different hairstyle for each day of the week. He must be feeling powerful today.

Doing as he says, I take a seat while unbuttoning my jacket, letting the quarters drape to the side. "Frank, how are you this morning?"

"None of those pleasantries. I want to know how the girl hunt is coming along?" He leans forward, his hands on his desk while he wiggles his eyebrows at me. "Do I get to pick someone for you?"

I chuckle, because honestly, it's the only thing I can think to do without insulting him. Every other reaction I have floating in my mind involves either cursing or potential violence. "Sorry to disappoint you, but I met someone."

"No." He snaps his finger across his body in disappointment. "Who is she?"

"June Lacy. I met her yesterday in the park." I want to tell him I even like her, she isn't just a test subject, but I don't want to divulge too many of my personal feelings to him. Knowing Frank, he'd use it to somehow make this "experiment" worse for me.

"Is that so?" He studies me for a second. "Are you lying to me?"

"What? No." I sit up taller in my chair. "I wouldn't lie to you, sir. We're actually meeting today at the park."

"Mm-hmm, and what do you have planned?"

"We're going for a walk," I answer lamely, my bubble deflating slightly. I wish I had bigger plans, but it seems like I'm limited with June.

"A walk?" He studies me thoughtfully, his fingers steepled beneath his chin. I have a feeling I'm not going to like what he says next. "Wes, do I need to remind you what the premise of this experiment is? I'm not sitting around waiting to read about you going on a *walk*. I want material, authentic material, and I want to know the steps a modern gentleman would take in order to develop a long-lasting relationship. This is going to be a how-to guide."

So no pressure at all.

"I understand that, sir, but—"

He holds up a hand, stopping me from continuing. "I don't want excuses, Wes. I want you to get it done. We've carried your advice column long enough that anyone could step in and answer your questions. You're replaceable. Don't make me get to that point. Got it?"

Well fuck me. And here I thought I was an asset to HYPE. I swallow hard as sweat forms on the back of my neck. The pressure cooker just turned up a notch. This is no longer an easygoing article I can write in my sleep. From the look in Frank's eyes, he's not joking around.

"Okay." I nod my head. "A how-to guide. I can do that."

Leaning back in his chair, Frank smiles, victorious in his heavy hand he hangs above me. "That's what I like to hear." He tosses a pen and piece of paper at me from his desk. "Take notes. This is what I want to see from you."

I quickly situate myself in writing position and wait for him to sound off his expectations. "I want to know how you met her, how you got her to meet up with you again, how you got her number." Yeah, still working on that one. "Your first date, communication between dates, what you send her, how you speak to her. Your rules about sex, foreplay, and PDA. What you talk about with her. How do you make her fall in love with The Modern Gentleman?"

Frank rises from his chair and paces a few steps before raising his hand to the ceiling, looking absurdly ridiculous. "I want men around the city, around the country, to talk about this ongoing piece, to use it as a road map to love, in addition to your advice column. Follow these steps and score yourself a partner for life." Leaning forward, Frank levels with me. "Make it impossible for women to say no to our tribe of modern gentlemen. And by no means are you permitted to reveal any aspect of this article or the column to June, or else you can pack up your desk. You should, of course, protect her identity, change her name, but I want this relationship to be organic, without any outside influences. Can you do that, Wes?"

Yup, no fucking pressure at all.

Shit, not only am I having to put my personal life out on the table for all to read, but I have to go against every honest bone in my body. One of my top rules in dating is honesty, but how can I be honest with June if I can't tell her details about my job?

Do I even have a choice at this point?

With my job security suddenly in question, I nod vigorously. "Of course. Not a problem, Frank."

"Good." He stands back and crosses his arms over his chest. "So, this June. Do you think she will be easily susceptible to your wooing ways?"

June, susceptible? True, I barely know her, but based on what I've seen so far, I'm going to say that's a hard no. Despite everyone else in the world wanting everything at their fingertips, June wants to *look up, enjoy what's around them*. It's admirable. *The world is a fascinating place. Soak it up.* She's unique. I think my modern ways are going to take a hit, but I'll be damned if I lose my job over this. June better buckle up, because she's going to be shot into the twenty-first century, courtesy of The Modern Gentleman.

Lying through my teeth, I say, "Of course, June is easily wooable. This won't be a problem at all."

CHAPTER SIX

D ear Modern Gentleman,
         During my transformation from a bro into a gent, I've realized
my vernacular is off. I swear a lot, can be crass at times, and still carry some
of the frat boy in my blood. With a new, professional job, I figured it was
time to grow up and trade the college sweatshirts for trendy cardigans. I
look the part now, but I'm having trouble when it comes to getting a
woman's number. Back in my college days, I'd just take her phone and text
myself, wink, and tell her I'd call her later. But after reading your articles,
I'm seeing that's not the best approach. Can you help a guy out?
      Sincerely,
      Numberless

                                                        Dear Numberless,
         Bleeding the frat boy from your system is going to be one of the biggest
   challenges you'll ever have to face, my friend. I'm guessing you're prone to
   chugging cheap beer, high-fiving like an asshat, and treating women like
      trophies rather than the beautiful humans they are. Hence you taking
   phones without permission. Total douchery right there. Here's sage advice:
   be up front. There is no fancy way to ask a woman for her number. Tell her
      you like her and you would like to talk to her more if she's comfortable

handing out her number. If anything, I preach honesty. Have confidence, be honest, and score those digits. You'll be pleasantly surprised by the kind of response you get.

Good luck, Gent,
The Modern Gentleman

WES

THE FEEL OUT

I f she doesn't show up, this is going to be humiliating.

Especially after I gloated to the boys about my luck.

I glance at my watch, trying not to look impatient, but as we move two minutes past our meeting time, I start to wonder if she was serious about meeting under this knotty tree, or what she refers to as the Wes and June Headquarters.

Fresh from work, I lean against the tree, one leg propped behind me, hands in my pockets, trying to be as casual as possible.

Yes, folks, this is normal, thanks for staring.

"Hello." I nod at an old lady who gives me a questioning look. "Nice day, right?"

"Pervert," she mutters, walking away.

Christ.

I stroke my beard just as I spot a wave of red hair bouncing in my direction. I want to play it cool and say I'm not relieved . . .

But Jesus, Mary, and Joseph, let's all hold hands and thank the high heavens she's here.

"I was beginning to think you weren't going to show," I say with a charming smile, trying to hide any evidence of doubt. Looking down at General Fitzbum, I salute. "General, nice to see you again."

I squat down and scratch him behind his ear. "Looking handsome as ever." Peering up at her, I smile. "June, you look beautiful today."

Compliments, men, did you see that? Simple, but effective. Compliment what you see. You're lucky the lady wants to meet up with you, so make sure she feels lucky she made the right choice.

"Beautiful, huh?" she asks suspiciously.

I swear, compliments are usually the key to success, even if she seems suspicious. Keep them coming.

"Yeah." I nod and stand. "Yellow is your color."

And I mean that. Wearing a simple yellow sundress, nothing too fancy, she looks beautiful with her fresh face, freckles dotting under her eyes, and her hair pulled up into a curly mess of a ponytail.

"Well, thank you." She eyes my outfit. "I see Mr. Fancy Hair stepped up his game." Straight from the office, I'm wearing navy-blue dress pants, a white button-up, tucked in neatly with the sleeves rolled up, and my brown, leather Shinola watch at my wrist.

"Sure you can walk in those shoes? What happened to the workout outfit?"

"Came straight from the office. Don't worry about me, I traipse around New York in these shoes all the time, they're worn in just fine."

"All right then, are you ready?"

I gesture toward the park. "Lead the way."

General Fitzbum starts forward and I fall in step with June. Luckily there is enough room for all of us on the sidewalk, enough that my arm occasionally brushes against hers.

"Warning, I like to ask personal questions," she says after a few seconds of walking side by side.

"Are you saying you're about to probe me, June?"

Her nose scrunches as she looks at me and I realize what I said.

"With questions," I say, my voice catching. "Are you going to probe me with questions. Not anything else. I mean, probing me in the park would be a first and I'm usually up for anything, but that might be too much for our first walk. Up to you."

What the hell am I saying right now?

To all the guys out there . . . if you're feeling nervous, don't ramble about being probed in the park. Ask her a question, get to know her. Feel her out.

"Maybe we can save probing in the park for a lovely Sunday afternoon if this goes well."

"Nothing says God's day like a good probing."

Just stop.

Stop.

Chuckling—thankfully—she says, "Is Wes short for Wesley?"

"It is. Wesley Waldorf Williams. My full name."

I can tell she doesn't want to be rude, but I can see the scrunch in her nose as she asks, "Waldorf?"

I chuckle. "The Waldorf Astoria is a special place to my parents. Enough said."

"Named after a hotel your parents most likely boned in? That must sit well with you."

This time I laugh harder and look over at her. "You know, I thought about our walk all day today, what we would talk about, what we would see, and I never envisioned you muttering the word 'boned,' much less using it in reference to my parents."

"I'm full of surprises, so look out." She nudges my shoulder. And even though I'm a gentleman, I hope she can feel the strength in my body, the muscles I hide under these dress clothes. From the way her eyes quickly scan down my body, I'm going to guess she can. "So what did you think we were going to talk about?"

"Not my conception, that's for sure."

"Then what?" She chuckles.

"You know, the basic get to know you stuff." I use my finger to count off topics. "Jobs, where we live, age, college, basic things like that."

"Ugh, boring. That's menial when it comes to getting to know someone else—just surface. I like to know what makes a person tick. I want to know what you would do if you were given a cantaloupe and a pair of nail clippers."

Please don't ask that question, as I have no idea how to answer it . . . carve it like a pumpkin?

"But if you must know, since you thought about it all day," she continues, "actress slash dog walker slash doll clothes maker slash occasional candy confectioner slash whatever gives me money. Bronx, twenty-five, and I didn't go to college." She turns to me, "Now you, and make it quick."

Surprised, I study her. "Doll clothes maker?"

"You'd be surprised by the demand for custom-made American Girl doll clothing. Moms want it all for their daughters. Especially here in the city. Woo." She blows out a steady breath. "One day at the Sunday Fair and I have a month's rent paid."

"Does that mean you have dolls all over your apartment as mannequins?"

"Pretty sure they stare at me while I sleep."

I chuckle at that while I envision what her place must look like. Eclectic, that's for sure.

"Now answer your questions."

Persistent, I like it.

"Writer for a social media platform, Central Park West, twenty-eight, and Columbia."

"Central Park West, huh? That would explain why your shoes and belt match so perfectly. It would also explain the middle name Waldorf." She playfully winks at me and then asks, "Glad we got that out of the way?"

"Relieved." Feeling out of my element, I dig deep into the playbook and attempt to impress her. "And I know you're itching to find out." I swallow hard. "Cantaloupe and nail clippers? What else is there to do besides carve out a statue of Sutton Foster?" I hold my breath, hoping she doesn't call me cheesy.

Halting General Fitzbum, she turns toward me with one hand on her hip. "Did you look up Broadway actresses today?"

"If I say yes, does that win me brownie points?" I ask, one hand in my pocket, trying to look as casual as possible.

"Maybe."

And that's how it's done, gentlemen.

Try to listen to your lady, as it bodes well for the future if you can impress her early.

"Does it help that I watched the cold opens for the past nine Tony awards as well?"

"Depends. Who do you think was a better host, James Corden or Neil Patrick Harris?"

Oof, a question I'm sure will lose me the brownie points I just earned if I get wrong. I scratch my beard for a second and then say, "You know, I'll probably be the unpopular vote here, but there's something about James that caught my eye."

"It's the accent," she says, joy in her voice. "Don't worry, it got to me too." She winks. *I think this is going well.* "What's something you've never done before because you're too scared?"

"Getting right in there with the questions, aren't you?"

"Best way to get to know someone, in my opinion."

"Fair enough. Hmm." I pause, considering. "Something I've never done before because I'm too scared? I guess that's easy to answer. I've never sung on stage before. And trust me, the world isn't missing much."

"So you're scared of embarrassing yourself," she points out.

"I guess I am."

"Makes sense." She turns around and walks backward keeping the leash behind her so General Fitzbum can keep plodding forward. "You're a handsome man, Wes. Very well put together with your tailored clothes, perfect haircut, and shined shoes. I'd say you care about your image, so it makes sense that embarrassing yourself is a part of the human experience you want nothing to do with."

"Does anyone like to be embarrassed?"

"I don't believe anyone does, but it's how you react to that embarrassment that sets you apart from others. I've learned over time how to deal with embarrassment, to not agonize over it, but to rise above it."

"Seems like you have experience in being embarrassed."

"That story is for another day." She smiles brightly and turns back around, letting General Fitzbum trot to a bench that overlooks the park's Turtle Pond, one of my favorite places in Central Park because of its serenity, overhanging trees, and of course, its turtles.

I walk casually up to her when she sits on the bench. I tilt my head to the side, one of my hands in my front pocket. "So, there's going to be another day?"

Sweetly, she pulls her feet up onto the bench, tucks her legs to the side, and motions for me to sit down. Gladly accepting the invitation, I take a seat next to her and drape my arm over the back of the bench while turning my body in her direction. General Fitzbum lays on the ground between us.

"Well, you did look up Broadway actresses . . ."

"Sometimes you have to reward a guy for wanting to relate."

"I appreciate that." She pushes her dress over her knees and says, "So you don't want to ever sing on stage, which is the polar opposite of me."

"But polar opposites usually work best," I say.

She eyes me, humor in her gaze. "Okay, when you have no obligations, nothing to do, where is your favorite place to be on a random Wednesday night?"

I look out toward the pond, watching the turtles from a distance. "Favorite place to be Wednesday night? Honestly?"

"Please. And no corny pick-up lines."

I'll tell you gents right now, when a girl wants honesty, you give it to her. You should always give it to her, especially when the atmosphere between you two is electrifying. Like it is right now with June.

There's something special here, I can feel it.

"Home," I answer. "I'd like to be home. And I know what you must be thinking. We live in the greatest city in the world with so much happening around us, so why would I want to be home?" I turn back to look at her, a smile tugging at my lips. "It's simple, I'm comfortable there. My job requires me to do a lot of research, especially when it comes to dating and relationships, so I'm constantly out with friends at trendy bars and new nightclubs, observing the masses. The loud music, the dark rooms, the cold hand from holding a tumbler all night. It's exhausting. Sometimes I just want to be home in a pair of sweatpants with a bowl of popcorn lying on my stomach and bingeing on Netflix."

"A homebody? That surprises me. From the outside, Wesley Waldorf Williams, you don't seem like someone who wants to spend his days lazing about at home, eating popcorn. You give off the image of Mr. Nightlife. Which makes me wonder, is Wes really the man he portrays, or is he a completely different person on the inside?"

"Only one way to find out," I say, holding my breath.

Her lips quirk to the side, her eyes bouncing back and forth between mine, playfulness in her body language.

Come on . . . she wants to find out, I know she does.

Hold strong, maintain eye contact.

Finally, she smiles and asks, "Would you care to meet up with me tomorrow? Same time and place?"

And that's how it's done, gents.

"Of course. I'd love to." Leaning forward slightly, I ask, "Does this mean you appreciate a man who can binge on Netflix?"

She leans forward herself and whispers, "I don't have Netflix, so I have no idea what a good binge feels like."

Leave it to me to find the only girl in New York City who still lives in the dark ages. Might be refreshing, since she won't know about The Modern Gentleman.

"You're an anomaly to me."

"I like to say a rare gem, a diamond in the rough." She winks and then looks at my watch. On a heavy sigh, she says, "I have to get going."

"Already?" I ask, standing with her and pushing up my sleeves.

"Yeah, I have dance class tonight." She pets General Fitzbum on the head. "Come on, fella, time to get you back."

"What kind of dance class?"

"Tap," she says over her shoulder and then twirls to walk back the way we came.

She's leaving like that? Not wanting to let this girl slip between my fingers, I say, "I'd love to talk some more, June. Can I have your number? Maybe we can talk tonight after your dance class?"

"My number? That's a big step, Wes. A step that seems too early, don't you think?"

Umm . . . no.

No, not at all.

That's usually the next step.

Pulling on the back of my neck, I smile and say, "Could be a good step, though."

She sweetly pats my cheek. "We can talk some more tomorrow. After a good night's rest." She waves her fingers at me. "Bye, Wesley Waldorf Williams."

"Wait," I call out as she walks away. "Same time? Same place?"

She spins, her dress twirling, her vibrant hair falling over her heart-shaped face. "What do you think? Bye, Mr. Fancy Hair."

I think I'm going to have to majorly step up my game.

CHAPTER SEVEN

D *ear Modern Gentleman,*
What's the follow-up protocol after a date? Do you call to wish her good night? Do you send her a text? How long should I wait? Three days? I've heard there's a three-day rule so you don't look too desperate. Is that true? What happens if I really like a girl? How long should I wait before contacting her?
Clueless

Dear Clueless,
Throw whatever rulebook you're reading out the window. Today's dating "rituals" have gotten out of control. If you like the girl, let her know. Nut up, straighten your tie, and call her. Tell her you enjoyed your time together and want to see her again. Tell her that night if you want, or even the day after. Whatever you do, let her know you're thinking about her. Women like to be cherished, not dicked around by the rules some meathead came up with one day while sitting next to a pool with a bottle of hogwash beer balancing on his stomach. If you want her, go get her. Easy as that.
Good luck, Gent,
The Modern Gentleman

WES

THE FIRST GESTURE

"**D**idn't think we'd see you in here tonight." Roman kicks out a chair from the table where he and Caden are sitting. "Did your rendezvous not go as well as you hoped?"

There's only one reason I'm sitting in this loud, busy restaurant in Hell's Kitchen with my friends right now instead of at home in a pair of sweatpants.

And that reason is my walk with June.

My short walk with June.

I order a glass of water, not in the mood for alcohol, and run my hand through my hair. "The date, if that's what you want to call it, went well. We clicked, she asked serious questions and I answered them truthfully."

"What kind of serious questions?" Caden asks.

I take the next few minutes recounting the fifteen-minute "date" I shared with June, making sure to touch upon her surprising questions, acknowledge her body language, and inform the boys how much I'm attracted to not only her looks, but to her offbeat personality.

"She's into me. I could see it in her eyes, in the way I caught her staring at me—but she was also very guarded. We hung out for fifteen minutes and when it was time to leave, she patted my cheek and took off. It was very strange, but I also somewhat liked it."

I really did like it, but sitting here now, recounting the date, my big question is, why is she so damn reluctant?

"Patted your cheek? Like a grandma?" Roman asks. "You sure she's into you?"

I sure as hell hope so.

"Yeah, she's different and I feel different when I'm with her. Almost as if I don't know what to say. It's weird." I lean back in my chair and rest my hands on my lap. "And I don't know what to do now. Normally, I'd text a woman, let her know I had a good time, and I can't wait to see her again. And if I was feeling up to it, I'd call her."

It's The Modern Gentleman way of doing things.

Date.

Text.

Follow-up date.

It's the perfect equation, and yet, it's not perfect for June.

"What's holding you back? The fifteen minutes?" Caden asks. "Didn't seem like a real date?"

"Maybe it was a real date, maybe it was a meetup. I'm not looking for a definition here. The problem is I don't have her number."

Roman snorts. "Seriously, dude?"

"Yes, seriously," I answer, exasperated. "She still won't give it to me, but we plan on meeting up again tomorrow, same time, same place." And yeah, I honestly liked seeing her today, but I want more.

"She should start paying you a percentage of her dog-walking money if she keeps this up," Roman adds like an ass.

Ignoring Roman, Caden continues, "Did you straight up ask for her number again?"

"I did. I asked for it so we could talk tonight after her dance class. Instead, she said we can talk tomorrow." Frustrated, I let out a heavy breath. "How the hell am I supposed to tell my readers to do anything when the woman I'm trying to date doesn't have a damn cell phone?"

"Yeah, that's hard. The only person I know who doesn't have a cell phone is my grandma," Roman says, "but that's because she uses a walker and refuses to be distracted by a phone. She has one of those emergency buttons she wears around her neck instead.

Pretty damn funny when I joke about pressing it. She gets all up in a tizzy."

"That's a dick thing to do," Caden chastises. "Don't mess with your grandma, dude."

"Eh, she says it gets her feathers ruffled. Gets her blood pumping in a good way. She's cool like that."

Wanting to bring the conversation back to me, I ask, "What should I do?"

Roman sips his drink. "Nothing you can do. You know next to nothing about her, and you don't have any means of contacting her besides showing up at the park at a certain time. Looks like you have no choice but to go at her pace."

"But what about Frank? He's going to want juicy details about how The Modern Gentleman works. How the hell am I supposed to conjure up a good article by writing about fifteen-minute walks with a dog named General Fitzbum?" I sigh. "By now, if it was any other woman besides June, I'd have her number, know where she works, and have a bouquet ready to be sent there tomorrow morning."

"Flowers are so cliché." Roman rolls his eyes.

"I didn't say flowers. I said bouquet, asshole."

"Okay," Roman says, rising to the challenge. "What kind of bouquet would you send June?"

What do I know about her? She doesn't seem to care for any kind of technology. Does she even have a TV? I want to say yes— she can't be that out of touch, can she? Let's see. She likes dogs, asking random questions, and is very outgoing. She loves the theater, is passionate about acting, and she looks drop-dead gorgeous in yellow.

Memories of her in that flowy, yellow dress, walking so casually, her hair flipping over her shoulder when she spoke to me, a glint in those turquoise eyes . . . made me want to know her better. Fuck, she's beautiful. And what makes her more enticing is her depth, what she really cares about. She couldn't care less about where I live, my "life stats," or what I do. She wants to know the bare bones of me, what's holding me all together. And hell, if that's not refreshing.

I've never met anyone like her.

"Dude, are you going to answer the question?" Roman presses.

Oh shit, yeah.

I clear my throat. "A bouquet of things to do on a random Wednesday." Yeah, that's a really good answer actually. Both Caden and Roman look at me as if I lost my mind. "It's a question she asked me today. Where is my favorite place to be on a random Wednesday? I told her my house, binge-watching Netflix."

"If I could binge-watch shows for a living, I would." Roman looks into his drink pensively, as if the job offer he's waiting for is floating in there.

"I think everyone would, man." Caden knocks his shoulder and then turns to me. "What would be in this bouquet?"

I shrug. "Random things. Mad Libs, crossword puzzles, popcorn, things to do that don't require technology."

"You see her tomorrow?" Roman asks. I nod. "Bring her the fucking thing. Maybe that will win her over and you can score her number."

Huh, he might be onto something. Look at Roman being a thoughtful fuck.

I sip the water the waitress sets in front of me as I eye Roman over my glass. "That's actually a pretty good idea. Have you been reading my column?"

The smile on Roman's face tells me that the next thing out of his mouth is going to make me want to punch him right in his perfect teeth.

"Man, I should have your job. You're whining about not having the girl's number and I'm over here making things happen." He pops up his collar. "Yup, they should start calling me The Modern Gentleman."

Called it. If I was my old self, my fist would be itching right about now, but I'm sophisticated now. I'll probably just "accidentally" trip him on the way out of the bar while hailing a cab.

That, gents, is not passive aggression. It's simply a condition of living in New York City where the sidewalk can be uneven. When you want them to be.

I'll give him a break though. Thanks to him, I'm thinking about the stops I need to make before tomorrow. I have a "bouquet" to create.

∽

Talk about obnoxious. This was a bad idea.
A really bad idea.
This is why I should never listen to Roman.

I'm standing in the meeting spot, feeling increasingly ridiculous with each passing minute as an obnoxious, large basket dangles from the crook of my arm. The straw monstrosity is full of all different flavors of popcorn, Mad Libs, crossword puzzles, and teal-colored pens.

I might have gone slightly overboard.

A bag of popcorn topples over the side for the hundredth time and I pick it up, shoving it into the basket, not caring about how it looks anymore.

Okay, I went way overboard. The basket is brimming with treats and I clearly didn't know where to stop. Desperation crept in last night and I ended up buying at least ten different flavors of gourmet popcorn from the specialty grocery in my neighborhood. In my defense, I don't know what she actually likes. I'd like to know, but I already know that would be a "menial" question and heaven forbid I ask one of those.

I run a frustrated hand over my face, wishing the circumstances were different. If I didn't feel pressure from Frank at the prospect of losing my job, I'd probably approach June differently. I probably wouldn't be as nervous, or scatterbrained, or clumsy.

I'd go at her pace.

Not feel the pathetic desperation to score her number.

I let out a long breath when I'm greeted with one hell of a

beautiful sight walking toward me, General Fitzbum leading the charge.

She's wearing a purple T-shirt dress, her wavy hair is piled into a bun on the top of her head, and her smile when she spots me stretches across her gorgeous face, lighting up her eyes.

Damn.

Okay, maybe I can be patient, especially when the girl I'm waiting for is June.

Pushing away from the tree, I greet her. "Hey, June."

She eyes the basket and smirks at me. "Really angling for that phone number, aren't you?"

I have to say, her teasing is fun. Quirky.

"If I had it, I could have called to ask where to send this instead of bringing it to the park."

"And where's the fun in that?" She takes the basket and starts sorting through its contents. "Teal pens?"

I shrug sheepishly. "They match your eyes."

Slowly, she studies me with a touch of skepticism before saying, "You're dangerous today, Wesley Waldorf Williams." She motions with her finger at my outfit. "Black pants and a black shirt, smooth responses. I better watch myself or I might surrender my number to you as a result of your seductive ways."

Chuckling, I say, "Black clothes are a weakness for you?"

"Not really. Most male dancers turn up to practice in all black. It's simply easier." She takes me in again. "But on you, with your muscles all ripply, and your broody eyes, yeah, I very well might be in trouble today."

Hear that, gents? A compliment, and yeah, it sends a jolt of hope through my veins.

"Good to know." I look down at General Fitzbum and ask, "How's the general today?"

"Moving slow. Mrs. Fitzbum ran out of his pain medication. It should be here tonight, but I don't think I'm going to take him very far in the meantime."

"Maybe he'd fancy a bone while we sit at that bench over

there and enjoy a crossword puzzle and some popcorn." I reach into my pocket and pull out a bone. No stone unturned today.

She chuckles and shakes her head. "Oh yeah, you're really on point. All right, let's sit down. I'm sure the general will enjoy the treat you brought him."

"And what about you? Think you'll enjoy the treats I brought you?"

"I actually don't like popcorn."

She takes a seat on the bench as my shoulders deflate. Who doesn't like popcorn? Isn't that a universal thing like pizza and ice cream? Everyone's supposed to like it.

I sit down next to her and hand General Fitzbum his bone. "Damn. You really don't like popcorn?"

Pulling out the strawberry-flavored popcorn, she pops the bag open and throws a few pieces in her mouth. "Nah, I love it, but I felt like you were on a bit of a cocky high there for a second. I needed to fish you out of the clouds."

Jesus . . . this woman.

"You sure know how to deflate a guy," I say while pulling out the lime popcorn and opening the bag, relieved. That could have been an issue since popcorn's my favorite snack.

"Deflate? Oh, don't be so dramatic. I just told you how hot I think you are in those clothes."

I grin. "I don't remember you saying *hot*, but let's talk more about that."

She rolls her eyes at me and points at the basket. "What's with the present? Besides the obvious issue of wanting my number. What's the theme here?"

I snag a handful of strawberry popcorn from her and say, "Remember our conversation from yesterday, when you asked what I'd be doing on a random Wednesday?" She nods, chewing on some more popcorn. "This is your random Wednesday basket. It's supposed to be a bouquet, but I got carried away yesterday so it turned into a basket."

"Crosswords, Mad Libs, and popcorn, that's your random Wednesday?"

"With Netflix in the background of course." I smile.

"Oh, of course." She eyes the basket again and touches my arm gently. "Thank you, Wes. This is very sweet of you."

Relieved she actually likes the idea, I try to play it cool and not get too excited. Hopefully by the end of our meetup I can score more than just another walk with the general. I turn on the charm, but not too much. "I wanted to do something nice for you, show you that I'm interested; I want to know you better."

"And you figured popcorn was the way to my heart?"

"I was hoping." I flash her a smile.

She nods, eyeing me. "It's a stepping stone. The bone for General Fitzbum was a leap."

And that was a last-minute thought. Thank God I trusted my instincts.

"Good to know." I nod at the Mad Libs. "Want to fill one out?"

"Uh . . . yeah!"

I hate to admit Roman had a good idea, it's incredibly painful actually, but that smile on her face, that infectious joy? Yeah, I should buy my guy a drink as a thank-you.

The worst part is, I've written about a gesture like this in my column many times, and yet, I had to hear it from my friend to remember. June Lacy is throwing me off my razor-sharp game. Once I get her phone number, all will be right in the world.

Her enthusiasm is infectious as we spend the next twenty minutes filling out Mad Libs, eating popcorn, and patting General Fitzbum on the head while he sloshes away, licking his bone. When she asks me for words, I can't help but stare at her as she eagerly writes in my answers. She's so damn lively, especially when she's having fun, and it transfers over to her beauty and appeal. Fuck, I thought she was pretty before, but when she's smiling, laughing, having a good time, she's downright sexy. I lean in toward her, wanting to be as close as possible, but being careful not to scare her away.

The Modern Gentleman never moves too fast, but when he does move in for the kill, he makes sure his woman knows his exact intentions.

As I finish reading her Mad Lib, I look at her and say, "You know, there are other body parts you could list."

"No way. Making you say boobies is too much fun." She snickers and then claps her hands together. "When you said something about throwing sixty-nine boobies in your mouth, tasting the color of the rainbow, oh God, I about died."

"Yeah, the people across the park heard you."

She chuckles some more. "I wish I had it on video."

"If you had a cell phone, you could have," I counter with a smirk.

"Cheeky." She leans back on the bench and looks at the sky. We stopped eating popcorn a while ago, and I'm pretty sure General Fitzbum passed out on the ground, snoring away. "Ever wonder what it's like to be able to fly?"

Did she say something?

I'm too distracted. I take in the graceful curve of her neck and the way her breasts push against the fabric of her dress. This woman has me ogling, something I always tell my readers to refrain from doing. No one likes a creepy perv, but fuck, I can't stop staring at her.

Her head whips forward, catching me as I scramble to tear my eyes from her chest and make eye contact. I swallow hard and nod. "Flying, yeah. That's fun. Wings and stuff."

What? Wings and stuff? *Jesus, man.*

She narrows her eyes at me. "Were you checking me out?"

Two ways I can answer this question. I can remove my proverbial tie, step down from my pedestal of The Modern Gentleman, and lie, or I can cinch that Windsor knot and practice what I preach—always speaking the truth.

"Yes, I was." I go with the latter, and there is no shame in my voice. I'm a man, she's attractive, and there's nothing wrong with telling her that.

"That's what I thought." She shakes her head and stands from the bench. She straightens her dress out and pats General Fitzbum on the head. "Come on, old fella, we have to get you home." Without another word, she starts walking away.

Uh . . .

Fuck!

I scramble to my feet, stuffing popcorn, Mad Libs, and pens back in the basket, and chase after her, panicking. "June, wait up. I didn't mean to offend you." When I catch up, I gently pull on the hand that's not holding General Fitzbum's leash. "I'm sorry," I say, hoping she doesn't hold my honesty against me.

When she looks up at me, I'm confused—what I'm expecting to see isn't what I get. I expect to see her eyes angry, fuming maybe. But they're smiling, light, playful.

Reaching up, she strokes my cheek with her thumb and fuck if I don't melt right there. "I'm only playing with you, Wes." Standing on her toes, she wraps her arm around my neck and gives me a hug. My mind barely registers what's happening long enough to wrap an arm around her before she's pulling away.

Another missed opportunity.

Pull it together, man.

She takes the basket from me as she steps back. "Thank you for this, it was very kind of you." Smirking, she adds, "It was also very kind of you to check me out. It's nice to know when a girl is appreciated."

I grip the back of my neck, still confused about what just happened. "Uh, yeah, anytime."

She laughs and sways back and forth with the basket bouncing against her hip. "Are you going to ask me out again, Wes?"

Despite her dizzying unpredictability, I want to see her, desperately. It's not just her appearance that has me begging for more, it's her ability to capture me with one question, one smirk, one grumbly nod from General Fitzbum. She's unique, unlike any woman I've ever met. And even though she exudes this perky, joyful persona, there's something heavy in her heart. I glimpse it when I ask for her number, when she bites her lip, wondering if I'm someone she can trust. I want to know why she tries to hide behind her smile. Just like her, I want to get to the bare bones of her soul.

"Are you going to say yes?" I ask, playfully.

She gives me a once-over, caution flashing in her eyes, even as she nods. "Yeah, I'd for sure say yes."

Another small, small victory.

Nodding, I ask, "Will you go out with me Friday night, June? I'd enjoy taking you on a real date."

She smiles. "I'd love to. I'm interested to see what you consider a real date."

And once again, the pressure is on.

"You won't be let down. Now hand over that coveted number of yours so I can call you with details." I hold my hand out and wiggle my fingers.

With a shake of her head, my rising hopes are smashed. "Let's meet at our spot at eight on Friday, and we can go from there." She presses her hand against my arm and squeezes. "See you then, Wes."

Taking off, basket in one hand and General Fitzbum's leash in the other, she walks away from me, once again leaving me with no way to contact her, just the hope that she'll show up.

I stare at her in confusion, a mixture of emotions racing through me. I like her . . . a lot, but this is getting frustrating. All I want is to be able to contact her, to be able to call her this week and ask her what kind of food she likes, where she might want to go, but I'm shooting blind with this girl.

I'm interested to see what you consider a real date.

Hell, I'm interested too. And I know my normal first date idea of a nice dinner is not going to impress this woman. I need to think of something creative, something out of the box, something good for the column that's also going to blow her mind.

The column.

Ah hell, I almost forgot about it. Anxiety rips through me,

causing my stomach to churn. I have to make this good for the article, but I want to make it even better for June.

At least I have a few days to think about it, while I memorize the way June felt with her arm wrapped around me.

I've never thought a simple hug could consume my thoughts, but it's only been minutes since she left me, I'm still trying to soak her all in.

Fuck, I'm in trouble.

CHAPTER EIGHT

D ear Modern Gentleman,
    I met this girl at the gym the other day. I've spent time getting
to know her, helping her with her workout, stuff like that. I finally built up
the courage to ask her out and she said yes. I high-fived myself right in front
of her, it was humiliating. Thankfully, she didn't hold it against me and
we're still going out Saturday. My question to you is . . . where do I take
her? I want to impress her and show her I'm suave and sophisticated, not
some gym rat who high-fives himself. Any suggestions?
    High-Fives Himself

Dear High-Fives Himself,
Cut yourself a break, as we all do something doofy at some point. The good
news is she said yes. This is where it gets fun. Finding the perfect date
shouldn't be scary or cause you stress, it should be an exciting challenge.
Think about what she likes, any commonalities you might have shared, and
then google that shit, man. The Internet and blogs are your best friend. Use
them. And don't forget to dress well, smell like a king, trim all the hair, and
serve first, eat last.
Good luck, Gent,
The Modern Gentleman

WES

THE FIRST DATE

"Your shirt is rumpled," Roman says, taking a seat across from me at my desk.

"What?" I push away from my desk and glance down at a pristinely ironed shirt. "You asshole."

His laughter carries through my office and most likely can be heard down the hall.

I straighten my shirt and scoot in, bringing my hand to my mouse where I continue to scour the Internet. "Glad you find that funny."

"Dude, I can feel your tension all the way from my office. It's suffocating." He pulls one foot up and drapes it over the opposite knee. "What's with all the stress?"

Glancing up with just my eyes, I say, "My first date with June is tonight."

"Okay, so what's the big deal? Take her to dinner, buy dessert, take her back to her bedroom. Let her suck your toes . . ." He wiggles his eyebrows.

"Keep your sick fetishes to yourself."

"Might not be for everyone, but you never know until you try it. I thought it was a no-go for me, but I'm going to tell you right now, the second go-around was arousing."

I pinch the bridge of my nose. "You have serious issues." Exhaling harshly, I turn back to my computer. "I can't do a simple dinner date with June. That won't impress her, nor will it impress the readers or Frank. I have to think big."

"And you're trying to figure this out right now? Doesn't really go with your whole 'be prepared' motto."

"You think I don't know that? Christ, man, I've been trying to figure out something ever since Wednesday."

"Really? That's embarrassing, man."

My head shoots up to look at my annoying friend. "If you're not going to be helpful, you can leave."

"I already gave you the bouquet idea, what else do you want from me? I offered up dinner and sucking her toes, that's the best I've got."

"Pathetic," I mutter.

"At least it's something. May I remind you, you have nothing."

Once again, Roman is right.

I press my palm to my eye. What the hell is going on with me? Dates are my forte. I've listed off so many date ideas I could write my own dating guide for singles in New York City.

So why am I drawing a blank when it comes to June?

Is it because I actually care?

Or is it the pressure from Frank?

Knock, knock.

Roman and I both look toward my office door.

Speak of the devil . . .

Frank points a finger gun at me, his nails painted black, his knuckles noticeably gnarly and bumpy. "Love the article so far. Wednesday night basket, clever, clever, Wesley. Keep up the good work."

Out of character, I give him a salute, and he takes off.

Before Roman can say anything, I say, "Please, spare me. I know it was your idea."

"As long as that's understood." He stands from the chair. "Let me know what you come up with, and if you revert back to dinner and sucking toes, I'm taking twenty-five percent of your next paycheck."

"Trust me, I'm not doing dinner and sucking toes."

I'm ashamed to say it, but dinner and sucking toes is falling in the lead with ideas as I walk up to the tree. I'm about five minutes early so when I lean against the tree, I pull out my phone and run through my date night ideas from previous column entries.

Dinner and a show. No, too generic.

Cook your own dinner. Needed reservations.

Picnic in the park. Need to get away from this GD park.

Shuffleboard—

"Buried in your phone again, I see."

The sound of her voice startles the shit out of me, causing me to toss my phone up in the air, only to have it land in a muddy patch on the ground.

Christ.

"You scared me," I say, trying to catch my breath.

She takes a tissue out of her purse, picks up my phone for me and wipes it. Handing me the phone, she says, "Maybe next time you'll observe what's around you rather than bury your head in your electronics." She tacks on a smile, and that's when I get the chance to take her in.

Jesus, she's beautiful.

Dressed in a cute red skirt that falls just above her knees, she paired it with a tight-fitting navy-blue top, and navy-blue flats. Her hair is wild with naturally defined ringlets around her face, and she's wearing a touch of makeup that makes her turquoise eyes pop like crystals.

"Wow," I say, dragging my hand over my beard. "You look stunning." I take my phone and stuff it into my pocket.

"Thank you." She smiles brightly and then taps my chest with her finger. "You look pretty good yourself. You wear a suit well, Wesley Waldorf."

"You're going to make me blush," I say, holding out my arm. "Shall we?"

Before taking my arm, she pats her purse and says, "As a solid warning, I have pepper spray in my purse, I am well-versed in the karate techniques of a white belt, and I know how to use my apartment keys as a shiv. Your chances of abducting me and going unscathed are low."

"Glad to see we've formed a line of trust."

She chuckles and takes my arm, her hand falling to my forearm. "Thought it was only fair to give you a warning. You know, keeping the lines of communication open."

"That's appreciated."

"So"—she bounces next to me—"what's on the agenda tonight?"

"Uh . . ." I freeze, my mind drawing a blank. "Well, you know . . . I have something great planned."

"Oh yeah?" she asks, skepticism in her voice. "And what would that be exactly?"

"Date things."

"What kind of *date things?*"

"Fun date things," I answer, begging my mind to come up with something, anything.

"Be more specific."

Before I can stop myself, I blurt out, "Dinner and sucking each other's toes."

She stops, her hand loosens from mine, and she puts her hand on her hip, a crease in her brow.

Damn it, Roman.

Laughing it off, I say, "Just kidding, we're . . . uh . . . we're going to play shuffleboard."

"Shuffleboard?"

Christ.

I swallow hard. "Yup, shuffleboard. Ever play?"

She looks me up and down and tilts her head. "I do," she says very slowly. "But you don't look like a shuffleboard guy."

She plays shuffleboard?

Of course she does. She lives in the fifties.

"Never one to shy away from new things." She takes my arm

again and I wrack my brain for any shuffleboard locations. The only thing that's coming to mind—surprisingly—is The Royal Palms in Brooklyn, which is pretty far from the Bronx. As we walk to the end of the park to hail a cab, I say, "Are you cool with going to Brooklyn?"

"Are you telling me you're going to take me to The Royal Palms?"

Smiling, I say, "Yup."

"I can't believe you got reservations. How exciting."

Fuck.

"Yeah." I gulp. "Let me check on those." I hail us a cab and as June gets in, I send a quick text to Roman.

Wes: *911, please fucking help me. Shuffleboard reservations at Royal Palms, half hour.*

Roman texts back right away.

Roman: *25% paycheck*

Wes: *I'll give you my left nut, just make them and beg. Please.*

Roman: *I prefer the right nut.*

Wes: *I swear to God, man . . .*

Roman: *Chill your dill, got it handled.*

"Everything all set?" June asks.

I stick my phone in my jacket pocket and smile. "Yup. Everything's great."

~

Roman: *Reservation is under CockDaddy69, set for 8:30, you owe me.*

Wes: *Are you fucking kidding me? Dude.*

Roman: *Call it your payment. Good luck tonight, CockDaddy.*

Fucking Roman.

CockDaddy69? Come on, man.

How the hell am I supposed to say the reservation is under that name in front of June without looking like a complete tool?

"I just love it here," June says in a chipper voice as we walk up to the hostess stand. "I love how they made the playing area look like an old cruise line. And then the black and white elements mixed in . . . it speaks to my old-school heart." She squeezes my arm. "You did good, Wesley."

Thank Christ for that.

Now to get over this minor hurdle.

"Hello, welcome to The Royal Palms. What's the name of your reservation?" the hostess asks as we step up to her podium.

So this is what descending into hell feels like?

My cheeks light up into a fury of heat as I try to come up with a subtle way of claiming our reservation. Faintly, I can hear the sadistic sound of Roman's laugh in the distance, envisioning me in this moment, savoring the embarrassment I'm about to suffer.

Pulling on the collar of my button-up shirt, I lean in close and whisper, "Yes, uh . . ." I clear my throat. "It's under . . ." Whispering, I finish, "CockDaddy69."

"What's that? I'm sorry, sir, it's loud in here. What's the reservation?"

I roll my lips together, trying to hold back my frustration and lean in even closer. Pressing my finger on the hostess stand, I repeat, "CockDaddy69."

"I'm sorry, we don't have a reservation for Cod Dandy."

Jesus. Christ.

"Is there a problem?" June asks, as a drip of sweat trickles down my back. She looks between the hostess and me and I shake my head.

"Nope, just some miscommunication." Voice coming out squeaky, I say, "CockDaddy69."

"Cold Bladdy?" the hostess asks with a confused look.

"CockDaddy," I say a little louder, as June moves closer, inserting herself in the conversation.

"Cotton Hammy?" the hostess asks.

Please, Satan, swallow me whole right now. Fingers pressed to my brow, I repeat myself slowly, "Cock . . . Daddy."

"Colton Faddy?

I'm about to grab her iPad myself when June yells, "COCK-DADDY, woman. C-O-C-K daddy. Like mommy and DADDY. Cock . . . daddy. He's my cock daddy. What a big COCK, Daddy. Cock! DADDY!" Calming herself, she turns to me and says, "Excuse me." She flattens her hands over her skirt. "Shuffleboard gets my gears going. What was the number that accompanied CockDaddy?"

Mouth dry, temples sweating, this moment beyond anything I could ever dream up, I say without blinking, "Sixty-nine."

"Ah, okay." She turns back to the hostess and taps her iPad. "That would be CockDaddy69. Thank you."

Scared for her life from the onslaught of cock, the hostess nods hesitantly and says, "Y-yes. I have you down on court five on the far end of the building. They should be wrapping up soon. Drinks are at the bar, food is offered at the food truck. Enjoy yourselves." She hands us a ticket, which June takes, because I'm basically immobile at this point. She leads the way, taking my hand in hers.

We make our way to the bar and take a seat across from our court while the other teams finish up. Not saying a word to me, June leans on the bar with one elbow and asks the bartender for two old-fashioneds before turning back to me with a smile.

"Hope you like an old-fashioned."

"Oh yeah, sure, love them." I swallow, a lump of embarrassment in my throat, my composure completely shot thanks to Roman.

She pokes my leg and with a smile, says, "That was a colorful reservation name. Anything I need to prepare myself for?"

"Heh," I awkwardly laugh and scratch the side of my beard. "About that. My, uh, friend made the reservations for me and he thought it would be funny. Sorry about that."

"No need to apologize," she says. "It livened things up. You know . . . since you were stiff the entire drive over here."

Because I had no clue if Roman was going to score me reservations or not.

"Yeah, sorry about that. Just . . . nervous I guess."

"Aww, you nervous about taking me out on a real date? Afraid I'll float away and you'll have no way of contacting me because you don't have my number?"

Uh . . . yup.

"Something like that." The bartender sets our drinks down and I give him my card to start a tab for us. I hand June her drink and say, "How about we start over?"

"Please don't make me introduce myself. That's always weird and awkward."

I chuckle and shake my head after taking a sip of my drink. "Nah, nothing like that. How about I start with this: you look beautiful tonight."

She smiles over the lip of her glass. "Thank you." She sips and then studies me. "You truly do wear a suit well, Wes. Very handsome."

"Is that so?" I flash her my best grin.

She nods, still studying me. "You're not my type at all, as I usually go for a more artsy guy. You know, the guy who thinks it's cooler to not shower than to shower?"

"I've smelled the type you're talking about."

She chuckles. "Not you, you're very . . . put together. Sophisticated, minus the whole cockdaddy thing."

"Tackiness courtesy of my friend Roman."

"Oh Roman, I like that name. Is he single?" She wiggles her eyebrows and when my mouth goes dry, she laughs and pushes at my leg. "I'm just kidding. Loosen up, Waldorf."

Yeah, loosen up, man.

I need to get my head on straight. I'm smoother than this, but the debacle of no reservations and then reservations under an absurd name has me frazzled, and I can't seem to snap out of it.

Deep breaths.

After another sip of my drink—or more like a gulp—I ask, "Shuffleboard, huh? What's your experience?"

"Well"—she crosses one leg over the other—"I've been an avid admirer of the game for years. Mrs. Fitzbum has raved about the tournaments she's played in, showed me pictures of her cruises, winning game after game—her glory days. I decided to try it out with my friend Phoebe. She knows all about you, by the way. You two could go at it about me not having a cell phone. Anyhow, we've played here a few times and I'll tell you, it's addicting. You're going to go home, dreaming about the tang and biscuit."

"The what?" I ask.

She scoots closer, one hand on my thigh. "The tang is what you use to push the puck, or biscuit, down the court." She turns so we're side by side, and then she points to our court. "See the triangle?" I nod, loving how close she is to me, her hand on my thigh. "You want to shoot the biscuit in there and score as many points as you can. You go back and forth, shooting against the opponent. It's rather thrilling."

"Will you show me the proper technique?"

"Of course." She squeezes my thigh just as our court begins to clear.

"Are you CockDaddy69?" a man dressed in a Hawaiian shirt and speaking in an Australian accent asks.

"Unfortunately, yes," I nod.

"Hey, nice to meet you, mate." He holds his hand out. "We're the Thunder Down Under." He gestures to a guy in a matching Hawaiian shirt and pink boat shorts. "We're your competition for the next half hour. Is this your girl?"

"Yes," I say, feeling weird referring to June as that. "I'm Wes and this is June."

"Ah, June, lovely to meet you." He takes her hand in his and kisses the back of it.

Now, listen. Modern gentlemen aren't Neanderthals when it comes to another man trying to move in on their territory.

No, we're polite, but we also subtly claim our territory.

Not pleased with Mr. Vegemite, I lift my hand to the back of June's neck where I subtly rub along her hairline with my thumb.

The guy notices and then quickly steps away. I lift my glass to him and say, "May the best team win."

"I'm sure we will," he says like a competitive moron.

When he walks to the other side of the court, June faces me and says, "Marking your territory, Wesley? Really?"

Shit.

"I'm, uh . . ."

She laughs and says, "Why do you think my hand has been on your thigh this entire time? There are three chicks in the booth at your ten o'clock who won't take their hungry eyes off you." She leans in close, whispering in my ear. "I get it, and I like it." Standing from her stool, her lips turn up as she says, "But don't think you're getting my number just yet."

She takes off toward the shuffleboard court and I let out a long exhale. I glance over at the booth of ladies and two of them wave at me. Standing from my stool, I give them a curt nod but then head over to June, who is already pawing through the tangs.

Maybe a week ago, I would have been interested in talking to those women, but not now, not when June is keeping me quite busy. And yes, I'm happy she felt she needed to make a physical claim on me. *That's one for the books, gents. Even if I don't know why she wanted to stake her claim.* God, this girl's unique.

"I don't understand what's happening," June says, frustrated after her turn. All her pushes have fallen short, something she's not pleased with. "On the other courts, I've had to barely push the biscuit for it to sail."

"Well, for what it's worth, the Australians are having a hard time as well."

"Their toilets flush backward. Of course they're going to have a hard time."

Not sure how that correlates, but not going to push her.

In moments like this, where I can see my date's frustration, I decide to take the easygoing route, make the most of the situation.

I grab a biscuit with my tang and I pretend to cock my arm all the way back.

"Cannon blast," I call out and push hard while making a blasting sound. The biscuit sails past the discarded biscuits, which didn't quite make it to a scoring point, and lands right on the top of the ten. "Hey, look at that."

June grabs my arm and cheers. "Oh my God, you did it. Look at you and your cannon." Yelling down to the boys, she says, "See that? CockDaddy is bringing it. Boof! Cannon blast, you koalas." She pats my back and then slaps my ass. "Good one, Waldorf, good one."

Ohh-kay.

While the Australians set up their next shot, I turn to June and say, "So what are the rules on reciprocating an ass slap when you do a good job?"

Drink lifted to her mouth, she says, "Not favorable."

I nod. "Good to know."

The Australians shoot, taking my tactic, and score seven. June is up.

She hops up and down, cracks her neck from side to side, and then gets in position. "Now what did you do?"

Ah, an opportunity to get close.

To get my hands on her.

Classic first-date move.

Take note, gents, this is how you get in those first touches while being coy.

Ever see the movie *Ghost*? Where Patrick Swayze comes up behind Demi Moore while she's using the pottery wheel? It's the perfect moment, the epitome of taking hold of a blessed opportunity to subtly move your hands over the object of your affection.

As I step up behind her, I can practically hear "Unchained Melody" playing in my head.

A master at work.

Watch how it's—

"D-oye," I yelp, just as June says, "Like this?" and cocks her arm back, shooting the tang pole directly into my unsuspecting and unprotected nutsac.

Man . . . *down*.

Hands to the crotch, I collapse to the ground, and curl into a ball, praying to Jesus, long-haired and Holy Jesus, that she didn't just pierce my nutsac open with the end of the pole.

"Oh my God," June says, falling to the ground with me. "Please tell me I didn't just peg you in the crotch."

"You . . . did," I grunt out, my vision going dark.

This is it, this is how I die.

On a shuffleboard court.

"Oh no, oh God. Are you going to throw up?"

"Chances are high," I say as pain curls up into the pit of my stomach.

Breathe. Breathe.

"Looks like CockDaddy's down," one of the Australians says, stepping up to us. "Want a lift to the bathroom, mate?"

Under normal circumstances, I'd tell these Bermuda-short-wearing nitwits to kindly fuck off, but when I'm trying to decide if it's sweat or blood I'm feeling in my nether regions, I give them a gentle nod.

"Sure."

Humiliation courses through me as each Australian grab me on either side, lifting me by my shoulders and legs, and carry me to the men's room, while onlookers point and stare and June trails behind asking if I need ice or a trash can or anything to help my penis feel better.

Balls. Not penis. Balls.

They set me down on a bench in the bathroom near the trash can.

"Sorry about your nuts, mate." They slap me on the back, toss up a "Cheers", and then head out.

I curl against the wall, the pain so excruciating I have no other choice but to lean over the trash can just as June pops her head through the door.

"Everything okay—"

A wave of nausea hits me, sweat breaks out on my temple, and just as I'm about to ask her to leave, my stomach revolts, and before I can stop myself, I tilt my head into the trash can and throw up.

I throw up hard.

CockDaddy just threw up on a first date.

Not sure this could get any worse . . .

⁓

"Hey, at least there was no blood," June says, hand on my back as I hobble out of the emergency room, wearing ice-pack underwear and sporting an old-man cane.

It got worse . . .

"Yeah." I grip the cane to help me walk.

Wish I'd opted for the wheelchair right about now.

After a wonderful display of throwing up in the bathroom, I asked June to wait outside as I went to a stall, pulled my pants down and examined my balls. When I saw my right testicle enlarged and colored in black and blue hues, I nearly passed out.

No man should ever have to witness their testicles as the size of grape *and* the size of a grape*fruit.*

Wobbly leg-inducing horror down below.

It took me a few minutes to gather myself and not pass out, but once I did, I wobbled out to June, told her I'd have to take a rain check on our date, and started to escort myself from the premises.

Guess who didn't want to leave me to lick my wounds by myself?

Yup, the ball-buster herself—literally.

Stripping my pants off and spreading my legs for a sixty-year-old ER doctor with a yellowed mustache wasn't exactly how I envisioned this night going, but hey, here's to unpredictability.

"I really am sorry," June says, for the fiftieth time. "I had no idea you were going to come up behind me."

If she'd watched *Ghost,* she might have had a clue, but I learned she hasn't seen that movie, while we waited in the exam room.

"It's really okay," I say, walking up to the curb. "I'm sorry we had to eat food from the vending machine as dinner."

"You know, I can't remember the last time I had peanut butter and crackers as a main course. But what a fine delicacy."

"Accompanied by your rendition of 'Seventy-Six Trombones' while we shared a bag of Skittles for dessert, it was quite the night." I laugh and shake my head while exhaling. "I'm sorry, June. This was not how I wanted to take you out."

"Don't apologize." She grips my shoulder. "Despite seeing you throw up and picturing what an enlarged ball sack would look like, it was a great night."

Leaning on my cane, I say, "So would you say I possibly earned that number of yours?"

She quirks her lip to the side while looking over my shoulder. "I don't know. Do you think you earned it?"

"Well, if taking a tang to the coin purse doesn't grant me your number, I think the pity handout of seeing me in an ER gown does."

She taps her chin, looking cute as shit. "That powder blue was very becoming on you."

"Not many people can pull off such a color."

"And I didn't have to use my pepper spray, karate skills, or keys as a shiv tonight."

"Thank God for that," I say, adjusting my stance, trying to alleviate the pain from the contusion on my balls. "If I'd had to run through the June Lacy Protective Gauntlet, I don't think I'd have survived the night."

"Not with the kind of hi-ya I can bellow," she says, pretending to do a karate move.

Chuckling, I say, "Terrifying."

She blows on both her hands and then shrugs. "Lethal weapons . . . not registered. But let's keep that between us."

"If I say your secret is safe with me, does that mean I get your number?"

"Resorting to bribery now, huh, Wesley?"

"Anything, so I can take you out again and wash away our memories of this night."

She presses her hand on top of mine and gives it a squeeze. "I don't know, it was a pretty memorable night. Could be the greatest start of a great friendship."

"Ooof . . . coming in hot with the friendship card?" I ask, hand to heart.

"I have to like you before I can love you." She winks and then digs into her purse. She pulls out a long scarf and wraps it around her head, making her look like an old farm lady about to let out the chickens. She strokes it and says, "Hate when my hair gets frizzy from the wind." Then she digs some more and pulls out a pen and a piece of paper. Hope springs in my chest. "What's your number?"

I rattle it off and then pull my phone out of my pocket. "What's yours?"

She stuffs the pen and paper back in her purse and shakes her head. "No, that's okay. I have your number, so I'll call you."

I'm in the middle of entering a new contact in my phone when I stop. "Are you serious?"

She smiles and waves her hand in the sky, flagging down a cab in no time. Opening the door, she steps off the curb and says, "It's more fun this way."

For who? Not for me. This is not fun at all.

"But . . . my balls."

"Yes, and I hope they're okay. I'll check up on you, don't worry."

"At least let me ride with you to your apartment, pay for your cab."

She rolls her eyes. "I won't give you my phone number, so do you really think I'll let you see where I live, Wes?"

She sits in the car and shuts the door, only to roll down the window.

"I'm not a murderer," I say, making myself sound more like a murderer than anything else.

"Oh, I know." She winks and then says, "Thanks for an eventful night." The window rolls up and the taxi takes off.

After all of that.

The tang to my thang.

The puke.

The hospital gown.

CockDaddy69, for fuck's sake.

All of that and no number?

I drag my hand down my face. There is no way in hell I can show up to work on Monday.

No.

Way.

CHAPTER NINE

Dear Modern Gentleman,
I'm going to gush, so bear with me. I had the best date of my life last night. Girl is sexy, funny, can tell one hell of a story, and she even shared her fries with me. Fries, man. I took your advice about grooming, given I'm a bit of a hairy beast, and she kept complimenting me on my hair and beard, not to mention how great I smelled. There was no kiss after the first date, because as you've taught us, holding out is better, but now that it's the next day, what's the follow-up procedure?
Fry Freaking Tastic

Dear Fry Freaking Tastic,
I commend you on holding out on the kiss. Even though I'm sure it was painful after such a phenom of a date, it's going to pay off. You showed your girl that you respect her and can wait. Huge brownie points. Now you're entering the critical phase, the follow-up. This is where you lay it all out.
Tell her how amazing she is, what a great time you had, and be honest about your intentions. Hey, I like you, would you be able to carve some time out for me this weekend? I'd really like to see you again. Let it be known where you stand; she'll be like putty in your hands.
Good luck, Gent,

The Modern Gentleman

WES

THE FOLLOW-UP

Mandatory staff meeting.

Three words put me in one hell of a mood this morning.

Still using a cane, I walk through the elevator doors of HYPE and onto a bustling floor. I spent the entire weekend in sweatpants, icing my nuts, and holding my phone close to my chest, waiting . . . just waiting for a phone call from June.

Can you guess? I got nothing.

Absolutely nothing.

You'd think that a deathly poke to the scrotum would warrant a phone call to make sure I'm okay, but nothing.

And because I'm a lucky bastard who can't seem to score a girl's phone number, I have no way of contacting her. So it feels like I'm back at square one.

Alone, numberless, with a serious case of black and blue balls.

"Good morning . . . oh dear, what happened, Wes?" Margaret asks, as she walks up to me, files in hand, a concerned look on her face.

As a gentleman, it's not polite to talk about my groin in front of lady folk, and knowing this, I decided to come up with a story to tell my co-workers that would help explain my use of a cane.

At least, I'm blaming it on the gentleman angle.

Let's be real. Who wants the notion of almost getting your balls punctured by your date to be the talk of the office on a fresh hell of a Monday?

I don't.

"Water on the stairs of my apartment, fell down, twisted my knee a bit. Thought a cane goes with my look better than crutches. What do you think?" I give her a charming smile even though deep down, I want to whack her across the knees and keep moving.

Can you tell my mood has shifted from delightfully happy to irritated ignoramus?

"Oh dear, that's terrible. But you're right, the cane adds a touch more sophistication to your look. I think you should keep it."

Over my dead body. The only reason I'm using the damn thing right now is because when I woke up this morning and stood, I felt too sore to trust my legs without it.

"We'll see." I give her a small smile and make my way through the office, nodding my head at people, but keeping silent given my current predicament. I make it to my office, collapse into my chair, and blow out a long breath just in time to see Caden and Roman stroll in.

"What's with the cane?" Roman asks, not bothering with a hello.

Thankfully, Caden sets a cup of coffee on my desk, and sports a concerned expression. "Did you play basketball without us?"

"Will you shut my door?" I ask, leaning forward to grab the coffee and wincing the entire time. Roman closes it and they both take a seat across from me. Gripping the coffee with both hands, I make my tone gravely serious. "I need you both to swear on your dicks that what I'm about to tell you will not leave this room."

"Oh shit." Roman shifts in his chair. "I think we're about to get a juicy tidbit. Can we guess what it is first?"

"No," I snap, wishing I'd taken my pain medication before I came. I was feeling better yesterday, but apparently all the movement today has made things extremely uncomfortable. To be honest, it feels like my right nut is about to pop from pressure.

"Dude, are you okay?" Caden asks.

I shake my head and steady my breathing. "Swear on your dicks, right now."

They glance at each other, then both put one hand on their crotch and the other in the air while simultaneously saying, "I swear."

"Good." I take a sip of the coffee, grateful one of my friends is thoughtful. "As you know, this past Friday I had my date with June."

"Oh damn, this is from your date?" Roman asks. "I hope you at least got her number."

Head still tilted down at my coffee, I lift my eyes up to Roman and the minute he sees it, he busts out in laughter.

"You didn't get her number?" he asks incredulously.

"She took mine," I say, turning back to my coffee. "She wrote my number down, patted me on the shoulder, and then took off."

"Oh man, that's amazing. A shoulder pat." Roman wipes away the laughter-inspired tears under his eyes. Can't wait to see what his reaction to my next news is.

"So what does the date have to do with the cane? Margaret said you twisted your knee."

See how fast news travels?

"Yeah, I didn't twist my knee." I clear my throat and continue to stare down at my coffee as I speak. "I took her to play shuffleboard—"

"You're welcome, by the way." Roman shoots me a finger gun and winks.

"Yes, thank you for making reservations under CockDaddy69. That wasn't humiliating at all," I deadpan.

"Oh shit, did you really?" Caden asks, chuckling.

"Anytime, man. I got you." Roman taps his chest, and I'm tempted to chuck my coffee at him. But I'm desperate for the caffeine nectar, so I keep it in my grasp.

"We got drinks, started talking, then it was our turn to get out on the court, so she was showing me how to play. It was fun. We were laughing, having a good time, and then June got frustrated because she's played before and her biscuit wasn't sliding—"

"Did you arouse her enough? You know there's no slick to the biscuit unless there's some foreplay." Roman smiles his pearly white smile and I sit back in my chair, wincing.

"Do you want to hear the story, or do you want to leave?"

"Dude, that was too easy. Her biscuit wasn't sliding?"

Caden looks between us and shrugs. "He has a point."

"Jesus," I mutter pressing my fingers to my brow. "I thought we were gentlemen here."

Roman laughs. "We all know that's a persona you wear; you're an immature idiot just like the rest of us."

Half true . . . I've been feeling more and more like that idiot ever since June came along.

"At least attempt to be mature. Christ."

"Sorry," they both mutter, but I can tell from the smirks on their faces, they don't really mean it.

Roman checks his watch and says, "Meeting in ten, get on with the story."

"Yeah, okay." Telling the guys is going to be just as painful as what happened. I can hear their laughter already, but I can't have them thinking it's my knee, when I think we all know by now what's really causing me this debilitating pain. "So, the biscuit wasn't sliding for anyone. My next turn, I really cocked back and threw my arm forward, scoring some points for us. June was ecstatic of course, and asked how I did it . . ."

"Ah, so you went with the whole *Ghost* approach," Caden says.

"I mean, who wouldn't?" I ask.

"What *Ghost* approach?" Roman asks.

"You know, showing a girl how to do something while coming around from behind so you can hold her while doing it."

"Classy move." He winks.

"Yeah, well it didn't happen like that. She had no idea I was stepping up behind her and before I knew what was happening, she cocked her arm back like me, sending the tip of the tang—or 'pushing stick' in layman's terms—straight into my right nut."

"Ohhh," they both say while cringing.

Roman grips his own balls.

Caden glances down at my crotch and then back up at me. "You okay, man?"

"I'm using a cane to walk around, what do you think?" I shake my head. "Had to be carried off the court by my opponents, threw up in the bathroom, and then sat in ER while an old man asked me to spread my legs for examination."

Roman is now laughing—so hard that he's crying again.

"I ended up with a severe contusion on my right nut—"

"Hey, that's the testicle you promised me in texts," Roman says with a grin.

"Well, if I don't keep icing it, it might shrivel up and turn into dust."

"Oh shit," Caden says, looking sorry. "Is it painful?"

"Let's just say my nutsac is enlarged and my entire groin and inner thigh is covered in black and blue, and I can barely walk."

"Oh fuck." Roman laughs some more and then says, "You have to show us."

"Fuck no. I'm not showing you."

Caden glances at Roman and the more level-headed of the two says, "Yeah, you have to show us."

"I'm not showing you my balls. Are you insane?"

"Dude, we've showered together before," Roman says.

"Don't say it like that, like we've shared an intimate moment. It was at the gym after a workout."

"Still, I've seen your junk before. And it's not like it's small, so you have nothing to be ashamed of. Just show us, come on. Drop your pants and show us."

"I'm not one to stare at other guy's junk, but as a man who is concerned of the same thing happening to him on any given day, I really need to see this," Caden says.

Why can't I have normal friends?

Then again, if Roman came into the office with the same predicament, I'd want to see too.

"Ugh, fine." I carefully stand while the boys lean forward in their chairs. It takes me a second to steady myself, but once I do, I undo my belt and pants, push them down to my knees, and them fold down my black boxer briefs, revealing the monstrous disaster that is my crotch.

The moment it comes into view, both guys make an unintelligible sound of disgust and shield their eyes.

"Oh my God," Caden says, almost in disbelief. He brings his fist to his mouth and shakes his head. "Dear God, no."

"That is . . ." Roman has his hand on his heart. "That is horrifying. Dude, how can you—"

My office door flings open, Frank pops his head in, and before I can drop the dress shirt I'm holding up, I hear, "Mother of Jesus, what is happening in here? Your balls, man . . . YOUR BALLS."

~

S ilence.

Sitting shoulder to shoulder, Caden, Roman, and I sit across from Frank's desk and are met with silence as he steeples his fingers beneath his chin.

It's safe to say everyone in the office is aware that in fact, I didn't twist my knee, but there is something wrong with my genitals.

That's a great way to start your Monday.

Another great way? Sitting in your boss's office, knowing he has the image of your enlarged scrotum burned into his skull.

I know this because he yelled it while walking away and telling us to be in his office in two minutes.

Frank lowers his hands and says, "What I saw back there—"

"Frank, I'm sorry," I plead, not wanting to get fired over an HR nightmare. "The boys wanted—"

Frank holds his hand up. "I don't want to hear it. If I was Margaret or any other woman, this would be a shitstorm right about now. Be happy I'm the one who walked in on your peep show." He groans and rubs his temples. "Why the hell does your scrotum look like that?"

"June," I simply say, which of course perks Frank right up. "First date."

"Say nothing more." He sits up, a smile on my face. "I can't wait to read about it."

"With all due respect, Frank, I don't feel comfortable—"

"Write it or you're fired. Simple as that."

"I'll have a rough draft on your desk this afternoon," I say with a fake smile.

"Perfect. You're dismissed." We all stand while he adds, "And from here on out, keep your pants zipped when you're in this office."

~

"A re you sure you're going to make it?" Caden asks me, as I hobble down the sidewalk in Central Park.

"I don't have a choice. She hasn't called me, and Frank is frothing at the mouth for more content from me after reading the deets on the first date." I pause and take a deep breath. "Fuck, I'm taking my medication when I get home."

"I don't know why you don't have it in your pocket."

"Pride. Stupid, stupid pride." I point with my cane to *the* tree. "That's it, I can make it from here."

"You sure?"

"Yeah, thanks, man."

"And getting home?" he asks.

"Might take me all night, but I'll manage."

He gives me a nod, and then I slowly but surely make my way to the tree, where I lean against it for support.

Stalking the person you went out on a date with isn't normal dating protocol, but as a man who can't seem to secure a girl's phone number, desperate times call for desperate measures.

And if I know anything about June, it's that she cares about General Fitzbum, and hopefully, she sticks to the weekday schedule for her evening walk with him.

One can only hope.

The temptation to take my phone out of my pocket is strong, but with my luck, she'll catch me "buried" in it again, so I keep my eyes forward, taking in the park and everyone who passes by.

I nod at people.

Smile.

Even pretend to tip my imaginary hat to an older couple, but regret it when the geriatric man compliments me on my cane and holds his up to compare.

Move along, man, move along.

I glance at my watch and realize she's five minutes past her usual time, and I wonder if she's going to pass this route or if she's taking a different one for today.

I scan the park, looking for bright red hair and a one-eared dog, and when my sight lands on a pair of green leggings and a white shirt being led by a familiar four-legged friend, relief washes over me.

Standing taller, wishing I didn't have to use the cane for support, I wait for her to spot me, and when she does, the most gorgeous smile I've ever seen crosses her face. She waves exuberantly and then heads in my direction.

Okay, so all that worry that she didn't call me washes away, as she comes in close and offers me a quick side hug.

"I'm so glad you're here," she says. "I tried to call you this weekend, but I left your number in the taxi. Gah, I'm so glad you didn't think I was blowing you off."

I scratch the back of my neck. "Kind of thought it for a second."

"Oh, so you're here to stalk me then?" She winks. "Nice touch, Mr. Fancy Hair. I like your persistence."

"Not creepy?" I blanch.

"Maybe, but I can appreciate it." She glances down at my cane and then leans in. "How's your . . . you know?"

"Painful." I nod. "Very painful. Please tell me you want to sit on the bench with me."

"I'd like nothing more." She takes my hand in hers and helps me to the bench. I feel like an elderly man who fractured his hip by the way I'm leaning on June and using my cane for support. "Remember," she says while I attempt to get comfortable, "the doctor said it's going to get worse before it gets better."

"Something to look forward to," I joke and let out a long breath. "So, you weren't turned off by what happened on Friday?"

"Not at all," she says, petting the general on the head before he lies down in front of us. "I was actually really mad at myself for losing your number because I meant to check up on you Saturday, make sure you didn't hate me. I was so distraught, I spent the entire weekend making doll clothes between auditions. I have over two thousand dollars' worth of frilly dresses in my apartment right now."

I laugh. "That's a hell of a lot of sewing. How did the auditions go?"

"They were great." She smiles. "One was for *The Music Man*. Can you believe that? A revival. I could not be more excited. If I can just get into the chorus line, my day would be made."

"I bet you killed it," I say, reaching out and tugging on one of her curls.

Now that she's here and she's not avoiding me, I have to move this relationship developing between us forward. I think back to the outline I made for gentlemen to follow, the specific step-by-step process for how to date and transform a relationship into something meaningful.

We had our first date, so now she needs to know what my intentions are. Normally, I'd do this over the phone . . .

Shyly, she places her hand on my thigh again and says, "I'm truly sorry about Friday. I feel awful."

"It was an accident."

"I know, but . . . you're in so much pain."

"I've survived worse," I say, like a man, even though I'm weeping like a baby inside, knowing this is the most excruciating pain I've faced in my entire life.

Drawing a circle on my thigh, she says, "So you being here, does that mean you want to see me again? Or are you here to let me down easy? And before you answer, I was really having fun with CockDaddy69 before the piercing of the penis went down."

"It was my balls."

"I know, but . . . alliteration and all."

"I can respect that." I smile at her. She smiles back. I feel like an idiot because I like her so damn much, and luckily for me, it seems like she feels the same way. "Can I be honest with you, June?"

"I would prefer it, but just sugarcoat the honesty. I'm not sure I can take a harsh letdown, as I'm feeling quite fragile at the moment."

She's feeling fragile?

I chuckle. "Even though Friday was the most unordinary first date I've ever had, I enjoyed myself, minus the ER visit. But even while we waited around, I have to admit, sharing a vending machine dinner with you was fun." I take a deep breath. "I like you, June, and I'd love to take you out again, but you're making it hard on me without a way to reach you."

"I know."

"And I'd really like to talk to you more, not just hope we'll cross paths in the park, even though it has a kismet feel to it."

"So serendipitous," she says dreamily.

"Very, but I'm not here to live out a John Cusack rom-com."

Her eyes widen. "Oh my heart, you know romantic comedies."

"I know a lot, which you'll find out if you take a chance to get to know me on a deeper level. What do you say, June? Can I please have your number?"

She taps her chin, giving it some thought. It's cute.

She's cute.

She's unlike any girl I ever imagined pursuing, but in an odd way, I'm glad Frank made me take this assignment. I'm not sure I would have met June, or tried to pursue her, after she had me hold her dog poop.

In a weird way, this assignment made me drop the constant rotation of life I've been living in.

Waking up.

Working out.

Going to work.

Researching at bars.

Rinse. Repeat.

It was like riding a carousel, but with June, I hopped off that carousel. Now, I'm riding a terrifying roller coaster that's also incredibly thrilling at the same time.

"You're killing me here," I say, encouraging her to answer.

"Fine, you can have my number."

"Really?" I ask, my brow scrunching in surprise.

"Yeah, you've earned it. You've shown true dedication, Wes." She chuckles and nods at my pocket. "Go ahead, pull out your phone. We can create a contact together."

"You've made my day," I say, retrieving my phone. I open contacts and click on new. She rattles off her number, helps me pick a flower emoji to accompany her name—her suggestion, not mine—and then she points out that she needs to add a picture so I know exactly who I'm calling.

She fluffs her hair and says, "How do I look?"

I'm holding up the phone to take a picture and all I can think is . . . "Beautiful."

She smiles at my compliment and I snap the picture. She's not looking at the phone, but at me and her smile is so natural that it exudes beauty.

"Is it good?"

"It's perfect," I say, showing her the picture.

"Oh, look at the clarity on that. Maybe I should get one of these phones."

"It would be easier on me," I say.

I dial her number and hold the phone out on speaker. "What are you doing?" she asks.

"I'm assuming you have an answering machine?" She nods. "I'm leaving my number on your answering machine."

We wait out the rings and then her voice sounds through the speaker. "Hey, you've reached June Lacy. Sorry I missed you, but if you'd like to leave a message, I'd be more than happy to return your call when I get home. Have a great day."

Her voice is so sweet. It puts me at ease, knowing I finally have a way to contact her.

"Hey beautiful, it's Mr. Fancy Hair. Just leaving my phone number with you. Please don't erase this message." I rattle off my number and then hang up.

She chuckles and bumps my shoulder with hers. "So what does this mean, Wesley Waldorf? Are we officially dating?"

"You tell me." I reach down and stroke the general's head, keeping my eyes trained on her.

"I think it does. I hope you're good at this." I'm cool as a cucumber on the outside, but on the inside, I'm fist-bumping like a teenager.

"June . . . I'm amazing at this."

CHAPTER TEN

Dear Modern Gentleman,
    I've been dating this girl for two weeks. She's so smart and sexy, I can't seem to find anything wrong with her. Dating her has provided two of the best weeks of my life, and one of the things we bond over is our love of cinema. But here is where my problem lies. She loves sitting in the first row. When I asked her about it, she said it's her favorite seat. What do I do with that? Who WANTS to watch a movie in the front row? I don't know if this can last . . . at least, I don't think my neck can take it. What would a gentleman do?
    Stiff Neck

Dear Stiff Neck,
    The front row? Man, that could be a deal breaker for me, but if you really like this girl, I think it would behoove you to have an honest conversation with her. Tell her you think she's amazing and she makes you incredibly happy, but the front row in a movie theater is for people with terrible time management. You're a gentleman, but you're also not a dumbass, and everyone knows the fifth row up, dead center is the best seating, and prove it to her. Make it special, get her a bucket of popcorn, bring a blanket if you need to, make the experiment unlike anything she's ever experienced. If you

want to keep her around, the gentleman would do his due diligence in
making it the best experience for her. And spring for the big bucket of
popcorn, don't be a cheap ass.
Good luck, Gent,
The Modern Gentleman

WES

THE WORLD OF DATING

"Why, don't you look handsome," June says, coming up to me in a navy-blue sundress with a yellow headband in her hair. She gives me a quick hug and then taps my chest. "Deep green looks great on you, Wes."

One of many things I like about June . . . she's not afraid to hand out compliments. She's always telling me how good I look, how I wear clothes well, how she likes my hair or my beard. She makes me feel good about myself. I appreciate that she notices the effort I go to so I look good for her.

"Thank you," I say, shifting in my black jeans and deep-green sweater.

"How are you feeling?" she asks, alluding to . . . you know what.

"Good actually." I hold my hands out. "Cane free. It was a long week, but I'm feeling pretty good. No alcohol for me tonight, though. I had my last pain medication today and mixing the two would send me for another visit in the ER. I'd like to avoid that for our second date."

"Smart." She looks around the packed bar and says, "Should we find a seat?"

I point to stairs in the back. "Trivia is on the rooftop; I already have a table reserved for us."

"Perfect." She takes my hand. "I'm excited. Was counting down the days all week until I got to see you."

"Yeah?"

She nods. "The general and I missed seeing you in the park, but I understand needing to heal."

"I'm glad I did, but now that I'm feeling better, I can join you for some of those walks."

"We'd like that."

I guide her through the bar, her hand clutched in mine, and when we hit the stairs, I lean close to her ear and say, "Stairs are difficult, so bear with me."

She chuckles. "Take your time."

After a steady trip up the stairs, I lead her to the table I have reserved, and when she sees our team name, she busts out in laughter.

"CockDaddy69?"

"I thought it was fitting since this particular trivia night's theme is on the adult side. Pop culture, sex, and dating."

"Raunchy trivia night?" She sits on her high-top chair and gets comfortable. "This is my kind of trivia. If it was history or science, I'm afraid I'd be lackluster at best, but pop culture, sex, and dating, sign me up." She rubs her hands together.

"And the food is themed for the night. The uncircumcised wieners sound appetizing."

She picks up the menu and eyes me over the top. "Your go-to is the wiener, when there's clearly toasted nipples as an option? Something I need to be worried about?"

Jesus, never thought about it that way.

"I'm not a fan of pecans, and they're sprinkled on the nipples."

"Ah, okay, so uncircumcised wieners it is, aka, pigs in a blanket." She peruses the menu some more and says, "This may be jumping the gun, but the Robert Brownie Jr. sounds delicious."

"I was eyeing that." I point to her menu and say, "And the Biscotti Pippen."

Her brow pulls together. "Biscotti Pippen? I don't get that."

"Uh . . . Scottie Pippen?"

"Who's that?"

I grip my heart and lean back in my chair. "June, Scottie Pippen."

"Yes, you can repeat his name as many times as you want, but it's not going to change the fact that I have no clue who you're talking about."

"Do you watch basketball?"

She sets her menu down and says, "I'm an aspiring Broadway actress who makes doll clothing for spare cash, does it seem like I'm a lady who enjoys dribbling?"

I chuckle and shake my head. "I guess not." I push my hand through my hair. "Does that rule out any dates to Barclays Center to watch the Nets?"

"No, I'm always open to new things. As long as you get me one of those giant foam fingers I see in movies. I think I could make it work."

"All right." I nod. "And by the way, Scottie Pippen was part of one of basketball's greatest dynasties. Michael Jordan's right-hand man."

"Ah, I know who Michael Jordan is. He was in *Space Jam*. Such a good movie."

Gents, any girl who thinks *Space Jam* is a good movie is a lock-down. Meaning, lock her down right away, she's a keeper.

"I think you just won the key to my heart," I say, making her smile wider.

"*Space Jam* fan?" I nod. "What about *Love Actually* and *Pretty Woman*? Those are my two favorite movies."

Not a huge romantic comedy fan, but thank Christ I've seen both. I have to thank past girlfriends for that, which I'd never in my right mind utter to June.

"Richard Gere is a hero in my eyes."

"You sure know how to say all the right things," she says dreamily.

We put in our order and luckily it comes out just as trivia

begins.

This is unlike any regular trivia night, which usually uses white-boards or even bells. This is trivia night on steroids. The emcee is a DJ, and she plays a great set while questions are asked, and food and drink is consumed. Each team comes up with a name and takes a selfie that is displayed up on a jumbo screen where the scores are kept and the answers are revealed. Every table has a keyboard that's connected to the screen so we can type our answers in, and like every other trivia night out there, no phones are allowed, which clearly isn't a problem for June.

"Let's get our trivia on," the DJ shouts into the microphone. Everyone cheers, including June, which I find endearing, and the first question is presented on the board. "What do Krusty the Clown and Chandler Bing from *Friends* have in common?"

"A third nipple," June says while biting into a wiener.

"Seriously? I thought you don't do technology."

"I don't do phones. I still have a TV and watch shows while sewing. Trust me, if I know anything, I know third nipples." She taps the keyboard. "Write it down."

Taking her word for it, I type in third nipple and sure enough, she's right. She gives me a knowing look and sips from her Melon Degenerous cocktail.

"Are you going to carry this team?"

"Just like shuffleboard, I think so."

And she does.

Question after question she gets right before I can begin to answer.

Kevin Bacon.

In a Cheesecake Factory.

Riverdance.

Six inches—don't even ask.

The car.

Harry Styles's high pants.

Eggplant + Taco = Squirt emoji.

Rubber gloves—yikes.

And here I am, just sitting, watching her casually eat while spewing off the answers, bringing us to the top of the leader board, neck and neck with Team Waffles.

"Clearly the answer is Beyonce's armpit. It's so obvious."

I blink at her.

Yeah . . . that's obvious.

"Are you sure?"

"Positive." She taps the keyboard again. "Write it."

I type in "Beyonce's armpit," and sure enough, it's correct.

"Ladies and gentleman, we are at our last question, and we're going to do this Jeopardy style. Everyone enters the amount they're willing to bet on this question; you can't go over what you have in the bank. Go ahead and type it in now."

"Put it all in besides ten points. It's a safe landing for us," I say.

"No, we should bet one dollar. What if we don't get it?"

I give her a look. "You just answered correctly with Beyonce's armpit. We are getting this one correct."

"Okay. Bet it all but ten points."

I plug in our number and once all the names light up green, indicating all answers have been submitted, the DJ says, "Okay, final question of the night. Fifteen percent of women do this on Valentine's Day. What is it?"

"Send themselves flowers," June answers while I say, "Masturbate" at the same time.

"What? No." She shakes her head. "Masturbate is not correct."

"You really think fifteen percent of women send themselves flowers?" I shake my head this time. "No, I did an article on Valentine's Day last year, and the answer is masturbate."

"Why would that be an answer?"

"Why would Beyonce's armpit be an answer?"

"Isn't it obvious?" she asks, as if I'm truly missing something.

"Uh . . . no."

She takes the keyboard from me and says, "It's flowers."

I take it back. "It's masturbate."

"Wesley Waldorf . . . it's flowers." She grows stern with me.

"June . . . uh . . . Marie?"

"July."

"What?"

"My middle name is July. June July Lacy."

"Oh . . . that's—"

"Odd, yes, but at least it's not the place where I was conceived."

"Touché." We both laugh, but then I grow serious again. "June July Lacy, the answer is masturbate."

"Ten seconds to enter your answers," the DJ calls out.

She tries to take the keyboard from me, but I block her and type in masturbate. "Trust me on this, June. We've got this in the bag. If I know anything, I know Valentine's Day. I've done extensive research on the subject. It's very common for single women to try out new toys on Valentine's Day."

"I really think it's flowers."

"Answers are locked in," the DJ announces. "Let's see those answers, one by one."

The board starts showing the team names and their answers, and dread starts to fill me as I watch team after team flash "flowers" across the screen until it reaches CockDaddy69, and in bright red and bold, "masturbate" is displayed. The rooftop erupts and the DJ plays an airhorn . . . several times, while our faces flash up on the screen, right under masturbate.

June buries her head in her hand while I nod and wave at everyone, embarrassment consuming me.

NOT correct.

Great.

When the DJ moves on, June gently places her hand on mine and says, "Thank you so much for mansplaining single lady Valentine's Day woes to me. It has really been enlightening."

I sigh and chew on the side of my cheek, wishing I had an ounce of suave left in me, but it seems like I tapped out when I met June.

"Should I give you back your number?"

She laughs out loud and then nods. "Might be for the best." But that teasing smile of hers shows me she's pretty easygoing, and even though "masturbate" was displayed above her head for the rooftop to see, she's chill about it.

～

"Sorry, I'm late. General Fitzbum was being difficult this morning," June says, coming up to our table, wearing a white dress and navy-blue heels. I stand to greet her, and she places her hand on my chest, lifts up, and presses a kiss to my cheek. She catches me off guard—I'm so used to her side hugs—that my entire body sighs with joy.

"Oh, look at you." I pull out her chair, and she takes a seat. "You look like you're about to go sail a boat. White pants suit you."

I chuckle. "The dress requirement of white and blue gave me the courage to pull out my white jeans."

She glances around the restaurant and leans in to whisper, "Everyone looks like they just arrived at the Hamptons."

"It's all a façade. No one who lives in the Hamptons would be caught dead at Boozy Brunch."

"Yeah, you're probably right about that." She claps her hands and says, "So how does this work?"

I hand her a mimosa and say, "Here is your drink and here is your drink card. The goal is to check off every drink on the card. Extra points are awarded to those who complete the challenges flawlessly. Food is brought around like dim sum, so choose what you want and eat as much as you want."

"What are the challenges?"

"That's the best part. You have no idea until you finish one of the small plates of food. The challenge is on the bottom of the plate."

"Oh, I like this." She sips her drink. "Bring it on."

Caden told me about Boozy Brunch the other day, and since

June is up for pretty much anything, I thought it would be a great way to have some fun and get to know her better.

While we start to drink and eat, I ask her, "Did you hear back about the auditions?"

"Not yet, but my agent said the directors for *The Music Man* were impressed. Fingers are crossed."

"*When* you get it, we'll celebrate."

"Yeah? You would want to celebrate with me?"

"Hell, yeah."

"Wesley Waldorf, you just made my heart flutter."

I smile at her. "You do that to me every time I see you."

She smirks and shakes her finger at me. "Uh-oh, are you aiming for a first kiss today, Mr. Fancy Hair?"

"I mean, I did wear my white pants and I'm getting you drunk. You tell me."

She leans in, her body language saying all the right things . . . her mouth, not so much. "I don't kiss until the tenth date."

Jesus . . . ten dates? Ten dates would be at least third base for other people.

"Ten dates, huh?" I gulp my mimosa down. "That's a long time."

"Isn't it worth it?" She bats her eyelashes.

I glance at her lips, and then to her turquoise eyes that are framed in a deep brown liner today. "With you? Yeah, it's worth it."

"Ooo." She moves away. "You're saying all the right things. I can tell you're determined, but just know this. You can compliment me all you want, there'll be no mouth-to-mouth today."

"What if I need to be resuscitated?"

"We'll cross that bridge if we need to."

~

"If I shaved your beard, would you have a dimple in your chin?" June asks, practically lying across the table. There is orange juice dripping down the front of her dress and unfortunately, there's blackberry jam smeared across my crotch from a croissant my drunk hands couldn't quite hold on to.

We are smashed.

I have no idea what time it is.

Pretty sure I've eaten my weight in breakfast pastries.

And I've lost all ability to pull from the gentleman's playbook. The only thing I know how to do right now is stare at the way June's cleavage is propped up by how she leans across the table.

"Boobs," I mutter, sighing as June's fingers play with my hair.

"I would find boobs?" she asks.

"I found boobs," I say, pointing to her chest. "You have boobs."

She glances down at her chest and gasps, as if it's the first time she's noticing. "My God, would you look at that? Boobs." She taps the table. "I have boobs."

"She has . . . boooooobs," I shout and point my finger over her head, like a neon sign. "Boobs, right here. Let's give this girl a round of applause." I clap but no one else joins in.

June holds her breasts and says, "Bet there's nipples attached."

"Oh easily. One hundred percent there are nipples attached to those boobs."

She sways to the side, jiving with the music. "Think there's a third nipple like Chandler Bing?"

"You should be so lucky."

"I have an overwhelming desire to pull one boob out and examine it, but something in the back of my head is telling me I shouldn't."

"Yeah, I hear that too." I look around. "I think . . . I think it's a mosquito."

"What? Really? You heard a mosquito talk to you?"

"Or was it . . . mojito?" I ask, looking up to the heavens for help.

"Mint Julep." She hiccups and covers her mouth, then laughs. "Black olives."

"Green olives," I add on, with a point of my finger.

"Maraschino cherry."

"What is . . ." I grip the table. "Excuse me, what *are* drink garnishes, Alex?"

June slaps the table and holds my hand up to the sky. "Winner. We have a winner."

"Goddamn, I'm good." I clap for myself and stand. Picking up an empty champagne glass, I hold it to my chest and say, "I'd like to thank the mosquitos for giving me the courage to be open and honest about my answers today. To the blackberry jam on my crotch, you might stain for life, but you'll always have a special place in my heart." June laughs. I chuckle too. "And even though it was tempting, I didn't say masturbate, even though it could have been the answer. I didn't say masturbate. No masturbating for Valentine's Day. It's always flowers." I tap my nose. "Remember that, gents, always flowers."

"Sir," a waitress says, coming up to my side, "I'm afraid your boozy brunch time has ended."

I nod. "Was it the masturbating comment?"

"I'm afraid so."

"That's fair." I hold my arm out. "My lady?"

June stands and wobbles on her heels. Gripping the waitress's shoulder, she says, "I know you're very concerned, but the contusion on his scrotum is almost fully healed."

"Indeed, indeed." I nod. "It's why I wore my tighter jeans. No chafing anymore."

"Really?" June asks. "Wow, what an improvement from sweatpants. Congratulations."

"Thank you." I bow. I turn to the waitress and say, "Thank you for your services today, you can send my award to the HYPE offices, care of, Wesley Mr. Fancy Hair." I motion my hand toward the door. "Shall we?"

"I think we shall." June hiccups again and then takes my arm.

"**W**hat the hell is touching me?" I scream, waking from a dead sleep and swatting at my arm. The quick jolt sends me careening off my couch only to fall flat on my floor. "Ooof."

Pain ricochets through my head as a deep voice says, "Good evening."

"What the hell?" I scramble to my feet, regretting that decision the minute my balls send a shock of pain down my leg, and my head pounds even harder.

Rubbing my eyes, I try to get them to focus and when they do, Roman comes into view, wearing a shit-eating grin on his face.

"From the look of it, I'd say Boozy Brunch hit you hard."

"Huh?" I ask, feeling something on my head.

Roman holds out his phone and shows me a picture of me. I'm wearing June's scarf around my neck, my shirt is on backward, and there's now red, green, and yellow on my crotch.

I glance down and sure enough, the colors of the rainbow are on my crotch, my shirt is in fact on backward, and I'm wearing June's scarf like an ascot.

"Don't bother trying to erase the pictures, I already sent them to my cloud. These are great fodder for future bribery."

I press my hand to my forehead. "I don't . . . I have no idea what the hell happened."

He points to a piece of paper on the table. "Me neither, but there's a note on the table for you."

"Really?" I glance around the apartment. "Is uh, June here?"

"No, but she was." Roman smirks. "And boy, do I wish I had been too. Seems like I missed out on a good show."

Oh hell.

I shed the scarf and shirt and walk into my bedroom with the note while Roman continues to watch baseball in my living room. From Chicago, he's a total diehard Rebels fan and, from the announcers, I hear his favorite player, Maddox Paige, is pitching. He's here until the game is over.

I'm about to cross the threshold of my bedroom when I call out, "Why are you here?"

"You texted me. Told me you were drunk and you were afraid you were going to do something stupid. It took me a few passes to read over your text to see what you were talking about, but seems like I was too late to stop the stupid train."

"What the hell did I do?"

"Just read the note." He lifts the remote and turns up the TV. "I ordered us food. Take a shower, your crotch smells like rotten cheese."

"Great," I mutter, closing my bedroom door behind me.

I shed my pants in the bathroom, turn on the shower, and then lean against the counter as I read the note from June.

Mr. Fancy Hair,

I'm drunk, but not as drunk as you, so please excuse my messy hand-writing. Since you are currently passed out, face up on your couch, I figured I'd take this opportunity to mention the following things:

1. *Mosquitos might be my new favorite drink.*
2. *Your booze brunch acceptance speech was the most poignant and insightful speech I've ever heard.*
3. *I appreciate the way you held my elbow the entire way home, telling me how much of a gentleman you are. I couldn't agree more. I've never had my elbow held so thoughtfully before.*
4. *You have great body. Like, really great. And I am a glutton for a little chest hair. Thank you for letting me run my fingers through it.*
5. *The lap dance wasn't necessary, but the extra condiments on your crotch were. Thanks for showing me what a genital rainbow could be.*
6. *You're right, ascots are for real men.*
7. *I might be drunk, but I will forever remember how you stood above me on the couch, squatted down like Magic Mike and thrusted your rainbow genitals at me. It's a moment that will*

never be taken from me, but instead, will be locked up in my vault of memories.

You are a wonderful host. Thanks for letting me pee in your apartment. And thanks for the show.

Talk to you soon, Wesley Waldorf.

XOXO – June July

Holy . . .

Fuck . . .

I grip my hair and pull on it. Please, for the love of God, let her forget every second of that.

Every goddamn second.

CHAPTER ELEVEN

D*ear Modern Gentleman,*
        I made a move. My girl was giving me all the right signals, so after dinner, standing outside her apartment, I kissed her. The only problem . . . she was going in for a hug so I ended up kissing her ear . . . with some tongue. I wet-willied her with my tongue. I didn't know what to say, so I bolted. It's been two days and I haven't talked to her. I really like her but don't know how to move on from something so embarrassing. Any advice?
        The Wet Willy Man

                                                              Dear Wet Willy Man,
  Oof, that's . . . tough. Let's call it like it is. That's an embarrassing moment that will be hard to move on from. The best way to handle it: own it. A lesser man would pass it off, joke it off, act like you were trying to do something else like pull a fly out of her ear with your tongue. Not a gentleman. A gentleman will go up to his girl with a single flower, hand it to her and say, "I'm sorry about the other night, for bolting and not calling after. But what I'm not sorry about is trying to kiss you." Be a man, tell her how it is, and my guess is, she's going to find the entire interaction endearing and you'll score that kiss sooner rather than later.

Good luck, Gent,
The Modern Gentleman

WES

THE ART OF VULNERABILITY

"I'm going to need you to dig deeper," Frank says, slapping Greg's draft in front of him. "Adult acne is no joke, so why are you making light of it? I want you to dive into the psychological torture of being a thirty-three-year-old man with a zit on his chin. Not spout off jokes about blackheads."

Poor Greg shrinks in his chair as Frank paces back and forth.

"These assignments are meant to give our readers a sense of community, to make them feel like they're not alone in this world where grown-ass men get acne, or pierce their nutsacs on first dates." All eyes fall on me.

Thanks, Frank.

I shift uncomfortably, staring at my iPad and praying for this moment to pass.

Frank moves around the room and with every step he makes in his Cole Haan loafers, my back tenses until it feels like concrete, just as Frank's hand lands on my shoulder.

"Take a note from Wes's playbook. He's putting himself out there. Playing the game, conducting a thorough investigation into the science of being a modern gentleman. From what I've read so far, his general outline of scoring a girl is not only riveting, but a winning product that will turn any single, uncultured man, into a devilish, drop-dead handsome, unforgettable gent. Swine to swan."

He raises his fist in victory. "You know, why don't you send everyone a copy of your work so far? Inspire them."

"You know, it's not necessary, I don't think it's—"

"Oh, it's necessary. It's raw and unfiltered, the way you describe the embarrassment of having to sophistically call out 'CockDaddy69' while holding your composure." Frank looks like he's about to cry. "It's what The Modern Gentleman is all about." He snaps his head to scan the room. "And I want all of you to deliver the same kind of product. Now get to work."

He claps, and the room disperses. I go to stand, but Frank presses his hand to my shoulder, keeping me in place. He sits on the conference table next to me and crosses his arms over his chest.

"What's next in the land of perfecting The Modern Gentleman's technique?"

"Uh." I scratch the side of my face and turn to my iPad, drawing up my outline. "The Art of Vulnerability."

"Yes, yes." Frank pinches his chin in thought. "How many dates have you been on with June?"

"Three, a few walks before that."

"Mm-hmm, and with this vulnerability tactic, what are you trying to portray to readers?"

I hate being put on the spot. Although, does anyone really enjoy it? Especially when I know so much is on the line.

My job.

My relationship.

My sanity . . .

The only good thing about the entire assignment is meeting June.

"Well, vulnerability and honesty is what I'm constantly preaching to our reader base. I want them to know that the modern man doesn't have to hide his feelings or his past behind a can of beer, but instead, he can expose himself, show his flaws, and let his love interest know that hey, he's human, just like everyone else."

"I see, and what makes you human, Wes?"

Let's see . . .

Getting wickedly hammered at brunch and pelvic thrusting my junk at the girl I'm dating.

That seems pretty damn vulnerable and human to me.

But I leave that out.

"The basics, you know. Afraid of failure—"

"No, no, no." Franks slaps the table. "I don't want the basics. What makes this article so real is the vulnerability you've already shown. Why do you think you've shown vulnerability?"

Was not prepared for the therapy session.

"Uh . . . well." I scratch the back of my neck. "If you truly want me to be honest—"

"Yes. I want honesty." He flaps his suit quarters open and leans in close to me. His goatee is inches from tickling my nose. "I need organic honesty, Wes. Fill my soul with your truth."

Someone clearly forgot to take his Xanax today.

There is no way I'm going to be allowed to leave this conference room until I dig deep and come up with something to satisfy Frank's appetite for the "truth."

So I take a second to think about my time with June. How she's made me feel. How I've applied all my techniques and failed miserably.

I run my tongue over the front of my teeth, suck in a breath, and say, "You know, I don't feel like The Modern Gentleman around her. I feel almost . . . out of sorts."

"Yes, this is what I'm talking about. Elaborate."

"I'm not sure, she's different. I'm anything but sophisticated. My techniques, although they seemed bulletproof, have slipped right past her. It took me one bruised ball and stalking her in the park to earn her phone number. Couldn't tell you what her lips taste like because there's no way she'd kiss me at this point. Not when she has a ten-date rule. And when we're together, I do stupid shit, things I would have done in college before The Modern

Gentleman was born. I'm so out of sorts with her that I find myself trying too hard and then failing miserably."

Frank stares at me, his fingers rubbing over his goatee. "Wes, is this . . . more serious for you?"

"What do you mean?"

"Do you really like her? Or is this just an assignment to you?"

Hell, the last thing I want is for Frank to make a big deal out of all of this, but from the look in his eyes, he's going to see right through me if I try to lie.

"Yeah, I like her."

He stands and walks to the end of the conference table and then back to me. He repeats that path two more times before stopping in the middle and saying, "This is more than I could have ever wanted. You are using each and every step to find love."

"But I'm failing with each step."

Frank shakes his finger at me, something he likes to do often. "No, if you were failing, you wouldn't still be seeing her. If you were failing, you'd be shit out of luck with this article. But you're following the steps and with each speed bump along the way, you're showing your honesty, your intentions. Isn't that what The Modern Gentleman is all about? Not being posh and perfect, but genuinely owning yourself?"

When he puts it that way . . .

"Yeah. That's what I constantly portray to my readers."

"Then you're doing it right." He claps his hands together. "Write me up some notes on what we just talked about. I have a friend in publishing. I think this would be the perfect proposal for publication."

"Wait, what?" I ask as Frank floats to the door.

"Publication, Wes. A book. You have a story, a guideline, and it must be heard, not just through HYPE, but through the masses. Who knows, maybe at the end of this, you'll have a book deal."

Before I can comprehend what he's saying, he walks out of the conference room, leaving me perplexed and in a bloom of excitement.

Published?

A published author?

Holy shit.

~

"And here I thought you weren't going to show," June says, walking up to me with the general. I was able to leave work early today, thanks to Frank's appreciation for my vulnerability. I changed into a pair of comfortable jeans and a T-shirt and then got back to our tree in time to find June walking my way.

There's something about seeing her floating red hair as she approaches that excites me in more ways than one.

"Why did you think that?"

"Not hearing from you last night after I left a note. I thought you were too horrified to show your face."

I move my hand over my jaw. "So you remember everything?"

She slowly moves her head, her smile growing wide. "You are quite the showman. If this writing thing doesn't work out, I could introduce you to my agent, get you some auditions."

"Weren't you drunk?"

"Not as drunk as you. I have a vivid memory of you thrusting your crotch in my face while saying multiple times how it wasn't hurting you."

"Dear God," I mumble, looking to the side.

She reaches out and takes my hand in hers. "I had a great time. Boozy Brunch will go down in history as one of my favorite dates ever."

She starts walking and keeps her hand in mine, taking me with her. "So, after getting an up-close-and-personal introduction to my rainbow and pot of gold, you still want to hang with me?"

"Oh yeah." She chuckles. "After that performance, I want everyone around us to know we're dating." We pass a couple on a bench and June motions to me. "We're dating. It's official."

"Congrats," the couple says, looking surprised.

"Thank you," June calls over her shoulder. "He has a great body."

My cheeks flame. "Please tell me I kept my pants on."

"Oh yes, pants were kept on. You did mention if you weren't still bruised, you'd put a thong on for me. I'm going to hold you to that."

"Only if you wear one too," I say, trying to lighten things up.

"What a grand idea. Screw matching pajamas, let's do matching thongs at night. I'll sew us some."

"Why do I feel like you'd actually do that?"

"Because I would." She smiles up at me and then squeezes my hand. "Seriously, yesterday was so much fun, and seeing you loosen up like that was the highlight."

"Do you think I'm stiff?"

"At times, yeah," she answers with full honesty. "But I see cracks in that stiffness and that intrigues me. It's like you programmed yourself to be a certain way, to have this certain persona, but when you're having fun, those cracks shine through, and I get to see the real Wes."

"I'm always trying to be real with you."

"Yeah? Then let's be real. Tell me something about yourself that scares you."

Did a convention on vulnerability pass through the city this past weekend and I didn't know about it? What is with the deep conversations from everyone? I know in order to move forward with June and for her to trust me more, she needs to see this side from me, but Frank too?

Twice in one day?

If I open up too much, I fear I'll find something I don't like and end up crying myself to sleep.

Although, one of the first questions June ever asked me was what I feared. This is her getting to know me on a deeper level.

What makes me tick is what she said on our first walk.

"Something about myself that scares me, huh?" I look down at her. "Are you going to answer the question too?"

"Of course." She pulls me to a secluded area off the path that I had no idea led to a bench. Trees provide a shadow canopy, and it's far enough from the busy path that it feels serene. We both take a seat and the general sits at our feet.

I reach down and scratch him behind his ear while June's hand falls to my thigh, her body angled toward me, her waiting eyes patient.

How could I not open up to her when her persona is so welcoming and comforting?

This feels easy, especially with her hand on me, encouraging me.

Leaning back, I drape my arm over the bench and say, "Honestly, I don't want people to think I'm a fraud."

"Why would they think that?" she asks, her nose cutely scrunched.

Without telling her too much about my job, or the assignment, I say, "I have to write about things at work that require research and sometimes it feels like . . . I'm just writing things to get the job done, rather than writing from the heart, if that makes sense."

She nods. "It does. Do you love writing?"

"I do. I majored in English, love all the classics from Austen to Orwell to Salinger. I have a mini library in my apartment, and when I say library, I mean a bookshelf I found at a flea market, a rich mahogany shelf with intricate detail. I keep my favorites on it. They're all bound in leather and look like they belong together, when in reality, all the words inside differ drastically."

She nods. "Kind of like people, right? Sometimes we can all start to look the same, following the trends, but on the inside we're all bursting with differences."

When she says things like this, it makes me wonder if she knows who I am, my persona at work. But she would have no idea who I am unless she did some serious investigative work.

Continuing, she says, "The differences are what make us truly special." Her thumb strokes my thigh. "I like your differences,

Wes, even if you find some of them to be embarrassing. They show your character, and I truly like the character I'm seeing."

"Would you say you're crushing?" I ask, trying to tease her.

She tilts her head to the side, her hair falling over her shoulder, her uniquely beautiful eyes shining at me. "You know I am crushing on you, Wesley Waldorf." She props her arm up on the back of the bench and rests her head in her hand. "What about you, are you crushing on me?"

Uhh . . . is she kidding right now?

If someone stopped in front of us and took a picture, it would be June sitting next to my body with a heart eyes emoji as my head, staring back at her.

"What do you think?"

"Hmm." She playfully studies me. "Well, you do like to stalk me in the park, you have no problem talking about your crotch or shoving it in my face, and you enjoy holding my hand." She taps her chin. "I'd say you're not just crushing, but you're crushing hard."

I chuckle and move my hand to her cheek, passing my thumb over her soft skin. "Yeah, crushing hard would be accurate."

"Is that so?" Her beautiful lips turn up into a grin. "So does that mean we're going to have another date this week?"

"I was thinking Wednesday. Are you free?"

"I could be. What do you have in mind?"

"Maybe something simple, something that won't put me in a position of total embarrassment."

She chuckles. "Positions of embarrassment make you real."

Well then, I've been the epitome of reality since I met June.

"How about a simple dinner? Nothing fancy, just a chance to talk?" I ask her.

"I'd love that."

"Shall I call you and let you know when and where?"

She nods. "That would be perfect."

~

"Hey, you've reached June Lacy. Sorry I missed you, but if you'd like to leave a message, I'd be more than happy to return your call when I get home. Have a great day."

I smile to myself as her answering machine beeps. So old school, I kind of love it—sometimes.

"Hey June, it's Wes. Just calling to let you know I have reservations at Mountain Bird on Second Avenue for seven. It's an intimate place, perfect for a simple night out. I'll see you there."

～

"I'll put your order in and be back to check on you," the waitress says, taking our menus and leaving us to ourselves.

Thanks to a connection at HYPE, I scored a table in the back corner, which is secluded but lit up by a brilliantly an old-school chandelier, casting the warmest glow over both of us.

June came to dinner in a velvet navy-blue dress that is skintight to her torso and flares at her hips, hitting just above her knees. She's showing more cleavage than normal, and her arms are bare, giving me a new introduction to her shoulders and petite frame.

"Is it that we're on an intimate date that you're smiling like that, or did something happen today?" I ask her.

She smooths her lips together, holding back her smile but then leans forward, and I have to urge myself not to look down her cleavage, to be a gentleman.

But it's really fucking hard, especially since this is the most revealing article of clothing I've seen her in, and she looks damn good.

"I got a part on the chorus line for *The Music Man*," she whispers, so much joy exuding from her.

"Wait . . . are you serious?" I ask, my heart stuttering in my chest. "You were cast?"

She nods. "Yup, my agent called me this morning."

"June. Holy shit." I stand from the table and come to her side.

I pull her up off her seat and wrap my arms around her. "That's incredible. Congratulations."

Her arms fall around my waist and her head leans against my chest. It's our first stomach-to-stomach hug and it's amazing, perfect actually, like she's meant to be in my arms this entire time.

And her perfume, Christ, it makes me dizzy. Sweet with a touch of a masculine scent.

When we separate, I hold her by the shoulders and look her in the eyes. "That's excellent, June. Wow, you must be incredibly proud."

Her smile is contagious as she nods and takes a seat. "I am. It's my first time in an actual Broadway production. My experience stems from small off-Broadway shows, which apparently has paid off. Gah, I'm so excited."

"Wow, that's really great," I say, reaching across the table and taking her hand in mine. "When do you start rehearsals?"

"Two weeks. Rehearsals are going to be brutal, but so much fun, and then opening night will be about six weeks after that."

"So in eight weeks, you're going to be tapping away on the big stage?"

Her smile grows wider. "Yes, I will." Shyly she says, "Think you'll be there?"

"Eight weeks from now?" She nods. "I better be."

"Would you tell people in the crowd you know me?"

"I hope I'll be able to tell people in the crowd that you're my girlfriend."

"Oh, is that so?" she asks, crossing one leg over the other and leaning in closer. *Eyes up, Wesley, eyes up.* "Ready to put a title on this thing we have going on?"

"I don't want to move too fast for you, but I have zero interest in going out with anyone else."

"You're just putting that out there?" she asks, her fingers gliding over my palm now. "So confident. You're making it hard on a girl."

"That's the point." I lift my glass of water to my lips while she eyes me.

"I think I can settle with the whole label thing, but not just yet. Let's see where the evening takes us."

"And you think you have it hard?" I shake my head. "June, you have no idea." She smirks, and it's a knowing smirk, as if she knows exactly what she's doing to me. I wouldn't put it past her. She's torturing me, and for some reason, I really, truly like it.

"Isn't courting a lost art?" she asks.

"For a reason," I suggest. We both laugh and then I say, "You know, you never answered your question from the other day, even though you said you would."

I can see her thinking back to Monday. "Are you sure?"

"Positive."

"Hmm, okay, ask me."

She sits taller and folds her arms under her breasts, leaning on the table, making her breasts more visible.

Torture . . . and she knows it.

I lean back in my seat and stroke my hand over my beard. "Did you come here looking fine as hell on purpose, only to torture me with how low-cut that dress is?"

The corner of her lip twitches. "I have no idea what you're talking about."

"Bullshit." I laugh and so does she.

"I must say, Wes, I'm impressed with your restraint. Your eyes haven't dropped to my chest once."

"I'm holding on by a thread here."

"Let me end your misery. Go ahead, feel free to take a glance."

I run my tongue over my top teeth, eyes staying on hers. The invitation is there, so do I take it? Or do I hold strong?

The gentlemanly side of me wants to hold strong, show her I don't need to look at her cleavage to enjoy the night. But then again, that alpha side of being a gentleman—where you show your lady it's not only about pulling out chairs and saying the right thing, but there's a naughty side to us as well.

I'd like to take advantage of that naughty side right now.

Slowly, I drag my eyes down her face, past her neck, to her clavicle, and land on her breasts. They swell past the neckline of her low-cut dress, hugging them together, making me believe she's deliciously naughty too.

When I meet her eyes again, they're no longer playful, but heated. I know that look. She's hungry, but not for food, for me, and for the first time since I started seeing June, I feel like I have the upper hand.

Studying her longer, keeping my eyes trained on hers, I ask, "Tell me something about yourself that scares you."

Her gaze stays focused on mine. She doesn't fidget. She doesn't show weakness. "I give my heart away far too fast."

Surprised, I ask, "Are you afraid you'll do that with me?"

She slowly nods. "You're too good, too suave, too on point with every move you make." Funny she thinks that, because I've been a hot-mess tornado, trying to make sense of this dating world since I met her. "You're intelligent in conversation, you're open, your honesty is unlike any I've experienced with a guy, and you're incredibly attractive. Almost feels too good to be true. I didn't think men like you existed."

"We do, you just have to find them right before they step in dog crap in the park."

She chuckles, her eyes squinting with humor. "If only I knew that sooner."

"Nah, then you never would've met me."

"True." She glances at the table and then back at me, a serious expression crossing her face. "Can I ask you something that hopefully won't insult you?"

"You can try," I answer, reaching out and grabbing her hand again.

"This may be stupid, but . . . you're real, right? This isn't some act you put on. Everything you've said, everything you've done, it's genuine."

"Yes," I answer right away, even though in the back of my head, my sub-conscious nudges the depths of my brain, asking if I'm being real.

I don't know any other way to be at this point. Before I became The Modern Gentleman, I was like every other guy fresh out of college, looking for a job, still invested in video games, and didn't know my ass from my head. It took time, but I've morphed into a man of poise, someone who generally knows how to say the right thing at the right time.

But is it an act? Something I automatically do? Or do I actually mean it?

With June, I haven't had to think about my actions, I've just responded. What she sees is what she gets. I guess I'm a combination of the two.

And it seems to be just fine.

"I'm real, June. Why do you ask? Have you been hurt in the past?"

"Maybe." She glances down at the candlelight between us. "It's why I take things slow. There's no need to rush for me. I'd rather get to know a guy, truly know him, before I give my heart over."

"I can understand that." Treading carefully, I say, "Can I ask what happened?"

"It's a tale as old as time," she says wistfully, looking up at the ceiling now, avoiding all eye contact with me, which leads me to believe one thing—she's embarrassed. "Met a director at a popular bar a lot of Broadway stars frequent. He made all the promises that I was going to be a star, made me jump through hoops, and in the end . . . found him with another girl, in our bed, jumping hoops with her as well." She shrugs. "You live and you learn."

"That's shitty," I say, letting the words slip out before I come up with something more refined.

"It was. I thought it was going to be my big break, but instead it was a huge setback. He played with my head, made me question my self-worth, and I took a break for a while when it came to auditions. A year and a half to be exact. It wasn't until recently I started feeling confident again."

"And look at what that confidence has gotten you."

"It's not a starring role—"

"But it's a start, and not just a start, but a giant leap into what you want to do. The experience you'll get is going to be worth so much. We all start somewhere, June."

She finally looks at me, a smile peeking through those lips. "We do, don't we?"

At that moment, the waitress brings us our food and sets it down. "Enjoy."

We both pick up our silverware and glance at each other. In that moment, I feel it—the *real* June was talking about. The connection, it's there. And I also realize I've missed this. This easy companionship, the person to relax with and talk about your weaknesses and your strengths. She's right to take things slow, because what better way to get to know someone without the physical aspect diverting your attention from the person themselves. So, we take it slow. There is one thing I know for sure—I don't plan on letting this girl go.

CHAPTER TWELVE

Dear Modern Gentleman,

Oh man, I don't think there's any coming back from this, but I'm hoping you can be a beacon of light. After three weeks of dating, I finally got my first kiss. And it was perfect, I swear fireworks were shooting off in my head. I was so excited that when we parted . . . I did a jig. I know. What the hell was I thinking? I wasn't. I blacked out and before I knew what happened, my elbow clocked my date right in the eye, mid jig. When I finally realized what went down, she was in her apartment with the door shut. Man, what do I do?

The Jig Master

Dear Jig Master,

I'm sorry, but . . . LOL. Gent, where's your cool? I get it, I get it, you were pining for that kiss, but if I teach anything, it's not to celebrate a major breakthrough. When you're home alone, that's when you celebrate. But we're too late for that. My suggestion: grab a bag of frozen peas, knock on her door, and beg for her forgiveness. Tell her that her lips captivated you, you've never felt anything so perfect, and you morphed into someone you're not entirely familiar with. Promise the jig won't happen again, and tell her if

she could give you another chance, you'd be grateful. *Still laughing. Sorry,
man.*

Good luck, Gent,
The Modern Gentleman

WES

THE FIRST KISS

"Are you coming to basketball tonight?" Roman asks as he enters my office, Caden following closely behind. He tosses me a bag of pretzels and then takes a seat in one of the chairs across from me.

"Have a date with June tonight," I say.

"Again?" Roman asks, sounding irritated. "That's the third night this week."

"So?" I ask, rocking back in my chair. "That's what dating is. We see each other multiple times in a week."

The past two weeks have been pretty awesome. After June told me about Doug, the director, we started to grow closer. I've learned that she's an only child, just like me, and she grew up with her grandma in the room next to hers. That's where she fell in love with Broadway, staying up late and sneaking into to her grandma's room, then watching musicals and rom-coms together. *Love Actually* and *Pretty Woman* were her grandma's favorites, leading them to be June's.

Her grandma always said Richard Gere, flowers in hand, leaving his limo and conquering his fears to be near his love, was one of the most romantic gestures she had ever witnessed.

Her parents never knew about June's late-night movie watching with her grandma, or they never let on about it. Her grandma passed away five years ago, which was a tough pill to swallow, since it meant she'd never see June on the big stage.

On the anniversary of her death, we watched *Love Actually* and *Pretty Woman* together. June told me every part her grandma loved, and I sat there and soaked it all in.

Every. Last. Bit.

I also learned that when June said she wanted to take it slow, she meant it. We hold hands and we hug, and that's about it. But the sexual tension between us has been rising and every time we meet up for a walk, June's regular clothes seem to get skimpier and skimpier, and so do her dresses.

"You can't spare a night?" Roman asks, as Caden just sits there, looking between the two of us, eating his own bag of pretzels.

"No. Not just because I don't want to, but because June starts rehearsals on Monday and I promised her one hell of a home-cooked meal before she goes on a strict diet, starting tomorrow. Sorry, man, find someone else to play with you."

Huffing, Roman shakes his head and says, "It's going to be your loss, your jump shot is going to turn to crap."

"It was never that good anyway," I counter. I have sub-par basketball skills at best. I play because it's fun, gets me out of the humdrum gym-life, and I get to spend time with my boys, but that time has been cut in half lately. I only see them at work now, and I sense it's starting to anger Roman. "Are you missing me?" I ask in a teasing tone.

"No." He pops a pretzel in his mouth from his own bag. "Just annoyed about always having to find someone to fill your spot. Eugene from advertising keeps offering up his skills and I'm telling you right now, the guy wears short shorts and it's not a good look. His penis popped out of them last week while doing a layup, almost smacked a guy across the face with his dick. No one wants that, Wes. No one."

I look at Caden to confirm the details of that story, because

Roman loves to exaggerate every chance he gets. He should have been the writer. Caden shifts in his chair and says, "I want to tell you it's not true, but unfortunately, it is. It was nasty, man."

"Then tell him to wear longer shorts," I say, trying not to envision Eugene and his mustache taking the court, whacking unsuspecting men in the face with a layup penis to the face. Doesn't sit well with me.

"Why should I have to be his dad?" Roman asks. "It's common curtesy to wear long shorts and underwear during a pickup game of basketball."

"That, and if you're hairy, shirt is always on," Caden adds. "No one wants to touch another man's shoulder hair."

"Men shouldn't have shoulder hair in general," I say. "Do they not read my grooming articles? I've written at least ten now."

"Surprisingly, not everyone in the world knows who The Modern Gentleman is," Roman says sarcastically. "I know that's hard for you to understand, but it's true."

"Hmm, I'll have to chew on that." I pick up my water and take a sip. "But if you're truly missing me, I'll meet up Sunday morning for some basketball. June and I are going for a walk, but then she's getting ready for Monday. I can meet you guys around eleven and then we can go out to lunch, on me."

Roman thinks it over. "Where we going to lunch?"

"Wherever you want," I reply with a roll of my eyes.

"Fine, but I'm going to need time to think about what restaurant I want to go to."

"What about me?" Caden asks. "Don't I get a say?"

"No," Roman says quickly. "So, get a kiss from June yet?"

"No," I sigh. "But I'm hoping tonight is the night."

"Jesus," Roman mutters. "I think I have secondhand blue balls just from listening to you, even though I had sex last night."

"Toe sucker?" I ask.

He shrugs. "She satisfies me."

"Bro, that shit is weird."

Roman holds up his finger and says, "I will not sit here and allow you to judge my sex life when yours is nonexistent."

"He has a point," Caden says.

"Oh yeah, and what does your sex life look like?" I ask Caden.

"Does a sex life with work count?" he asks, wincing.

Roman and I both exchange glances and say "no" at the same time.

"Thought I'd try." He chuckles to himself. "But if you must know, Roman switched the CockDaddy69 profile over to me, and I've been chatting with some women. No toe suckers"—he crosses his fingers—"but here's hoping."

"You won't regret it, trust me." Roman looks off into the distance dreamily and I wonder what the hell is wrong with him.

"Meeting boys, meeting," Frank says, knocking on my door. "We have plenty of things to discuss and I want to hear more about this toe sucking."

"Ah hell," Roman mutters once Frank walks away. "I swear to Christ Himself, if Frank suggests I write an article on toe sucking, I'm quitting."

"He wouldn't, you're not a writer."

Roman gives me a look as we all stand and head for the door. "Yeah, that's what you said when he asked me to write a five-hundred-word article on the meaning of hot sauce. What the hell was that?"

I laugh—I'd completely forgotten about that. Frank was trying to test everyone on staff to see if they could add content.

"I don't know, but your approach was genius."

"What is Frank's Hot Sauce?" Roman laughs. "He didn't appreciate me talking about his lady friends and referring to them as sauce."

"I sure as hell did."

≈

"I knew you were going to have a nice place," June says, as she takes my apartment in. "I barely remember it from my drunken visit last time."

I have a modest one-bedroom in an older building right off Central Park West. I don't have a beautiful view of the greenery that's right outside my apartment, but it's spacious enough that I don't feel claustrophobic when I'm at home. I feel comfortable.

And with June in my apartment, I feel even more comfortable.

She spins around to face me, wearing a pair of leggings and a cropped sweater that falls off her shoulder. She's casual, but stunning at the same time. I told her there was no need to dress up tonight, that we were going to keep it simple at my apartment. But her simple is a step up, that's for damn sure.

"Thank you."

She looks over her shoulder, smiles, and walks over to my bookshelf, where she hinges at the waist and runs her finger over the bindings of all my books.

"You do have a lot, don't you?" She studies them. "Would you hate me if I said I haven't read three quarters of these?"

"No," I say, sticking my hands in my jeans pockets. "You have plenty of life left to catch up."

"Good answer," she says and then pulls a book out. From its color and thickness, I can tell she pulled *Little Women*. Her hand smoothly runs over the cover and she asks, "Do you actually read these or are they just for looking at?"

"A book is supposed to be read, so what do you think?"

"I think you're crazy for bending these beautiful bindings."

I walk over to her and pick up *The Catcher in the Rye*, examining it as well. "I'm careful with the things I cherish."

She glances at me, catching the seriousness in my eyes. She blows out a quick breath and puts the book back on the shelf. "Once again, the man comes prepared to woo the girl. Looking for that first kiss tonight, Mr. Fancy Hair?"

"Might have crossed my mind a few times."

Or maybe every minute of the day leading up to this moment.

"I'm holding out to see how these steaks of yours taste."

Coming up from behind her, I wrap my arms around her waist and rest my chin on her shoulder. It's a new embrace for us, and I stand still for a second, waiting for her to grow stiff and push me away, but instead, she lolls her head to the side, lifts her arm, and sifts her hand through my hair.

Jesus Christ, that feels good, her hand in my hair. It's a simple touch, one I've definitely taken advantage of before. But right now, I'm committing this feeling to memory.

My hand skims across her bare stomach and when she turns in my arms to face me, my breath catches when her hands fall to my shoulders, her eyes staring up at me.

"Yeah," she sighs. "You're incredibly dangerous tonight."

"Nah, not dangerous, just invested. I like you a lot, and I want you to know that." And because she also needs to know I'm a man who takes control, I slide my hand under the back of her cropped sweater and splay it across her back, my fingers dancing across the clasp of her bra. She sucks in a sharp breath and moves her hands to my neck and jaw.

Is this it? Is she going to kiss me right now?

We've had ten dates.

Trust me, I've counted.

Could tonight finally be it?

Can you tell I'm desperate?

But knowing my luck where this girl is concerned, I'm going to say a kiss tonight is a far-fetched idea. I've thought she was going to kiss me many times over the past two weeks, and every time she walked away, I felt a piece of me wilt like the damn flower in *Beauty and the Beast.*

"I like you a lot too, Wes," she says, seriously. "I actually told my parents about you yesterday."

"You did?" I ask, holding on to her, keeping her close as we stand in the middle of my apartment. "What did you say?"

"Well . . ." Her fingers stroke the back of my neck. "I told them

I met this guy while walking the general, that he almost stepped in dog crap, but I saved him from having to scrub his shoes clean. And after berating him for being so engrossed in his phone, I told them I couldn't stop staring at him and how good-looking he was."

"Did you tell them how you swooned so hard I had to catch you as you teetered to the ground?"

"Yup, told them that, sure," she answers sarcastically and then laughs. "I told them you're a writer and you like popcorn, which they love by the way. And I told them that you like to be referred to as CockDaddy69."

"No, you didn't."

"My dad thought it was a brutally honest name and respected you for it."

"June, be serious."

"I am." She twirls her finger on the back of my neck. "When I showed them a picture of you, my mom said, 'oh yeah, he's a cock daddy, all right.'"

I pause, tying to gauge how serious she is, but when she doesn't crack into laughter, I think she's telling the truth.

"June . . ."

"Yes?" She bats her eyelashes.

"Did you really refer to me as CockDaddy69 to your parents?"

"I did." Her hands move forward to my cheeks and her body inches forward, her pelvis against mine. "Is that a problem?"

I swallow hard, trying to find my voice. Having her this close, when I've been craving her for so damn long, makes my mind melt into nothing as I simply feel.

Feel how her breasts graze my chest.

How she stands on her toes to be close to me.

How her hands cup my cheeks, pulling my head closer to hers.

How she licks her lips and then glances at mine.

Fuck . . .

She wants a kiss.

Right here.

Right fucking now.

My hands slide up her back and I lean closer—so close I can practically taste her.

"Do you want this?" I ask, forgetting all about CockDaddy and her parents.

"I do," she replies. "I . . . what's that smell?"

"I sprayed some cologne before you got here." I lean in closer, licking my lips, and just as I descend, going in for our first kiss, I close my eyes, pucker up, and . . .

"No, what's that burning smell?" she asks, her head whipping to the side, just in time for my lips to open-mouth kiss her ear.

Her actual . . . ear.

Lips to hearing organ.

Mouth crashing against pinna and canal.

Oh dear . . . *God.*

"Ah, that's wet." She wipes her ear frantically with her shoulder and my mind immediately falls to the wet willy reader.

Did I just give June a wet willy?

No, there was no tongue. Just lips.

Either way, humiliation washes over me as I try to think of what to say.

Anything.

Think of anything that would ease the awkwardness of this moment.

She continues to wipe at her ear. Good God, it's not like I spit in it? Why is she still wiping?

Wait, focus. Say something.

Something smart.

Witty.

Something that won't make me look like a moron.

"Your ear . . . I uh." I pull on the back of my neck. "I find it very attractive."

Gents, please look away. Please, for the love of God, just look away and stop taking notes. This is a moment I'd like to collectively as a whole, forget about.

"What?" She gives me a lost look. "Wes, did you hear me? I think something is burning in your kitchen."

"Wait, what?" And that's when the burning smell hits me. "Oh fuck, I'm broiling the steak and potatoes for an added crisp."

I sprint to the kitchen just in time to see flames coming from the oven.

"Oh fuck. Oh FUCK," I say louder, dancing in place. "June, I need the—"

In a matter of seconds, as I spin toward June, the fire alarm in the kitchen goes off, sending a shrill screech through my apartment.

Blinded by the sound, I'm unaware that June is holding a red canister in hand. And right on time, I'm blasted in the face with fire retardant from the extinguisher I keep on the wall of my kitchen. *Poof!*

While gaining my bearings, the fire sprinklers, which were just installed in our building, thanks to the new law passed in New York City, spring out of their sockets and douse the kitchen in water, drenching me and our dinner.

"Fire extinguisher," I finish, swiping my eyes clean only to find June standing in front of me, a shocked look on her face, completely dry somehow, and holding the fire extinguisher like she's about to go into battle.

"Oh my God," she breathes.

"Quick on the trigger there, June."

Still shocked, she blinks a few times and says, "That was . . . wow . . . you know, I don't think we can eat those steaks now."

I chuckle and shake the extinguisher off me just as the sprinklers stop and the fire alarm ceases. "How do you feel about pizza?"

"Do you mind pineapple and ham?" she asks with a slight wince.

"Anything you want, June. Anything you want."

"I love the way your soap smells," June says, as her legs are draped across mine, her back up against the arm of my couch.

We're sitting incredibly close. Pizza's been consumed, dessert too—thankfully saved from the rain, since the pudding I'd made was in the fridge chilling—and we're listening to the Jonas Brothers while talking. Yes, the Jonas Brothers—June has accepted my love for them and now hums along to the songs. Catchy and fulfilling, the only way to describe them. I couldn't think of a better way to spend a Friday night, well . . . minus the whole fire extinguisher and sprinklers thing.

June was awesome, because while I ordered the pizza then showered, she mopped up my kitchen and disposed of the charred food. I dressed in a pair of sweats and a T-shirt after that, and we've spent the rest of the evening exactly like this.

"Thanks. We got these soap samples at work and I was the tester. It's called Man Soap. It was developed by this guy in Los Angeles. What was his name?" I think about it for a second. "It was a type of beer . . . oh, Porter. Porter Smith. Pretty decent guy. He came to New York to pitch the product with his wife, Marley. Said they made a road trip of it. Apparently, that's their thing."

"Well, it smells amazing." June leans closer and brings her nose to the side of my neck, sending chills down my arm. "Really good. Maybe I need to get myself some Man Soap."

"Completely eco-friendly too, if you're into that."

"I am." She nods. "I like the earth."

"What else do you like?" I ask. My arm drapes over her shoulders, and we're our own personal human pretzel as we sit on my couch.

Comfortable. That's the only way I can describe this feeling. Absolutely comfortable.

"Hmm, what else do I like? Well, humpback whales are my favorite."

Random, but one of the reasons I like her so much.

"Humpback whales are legit."

She leans her head against my arm and gazes into my eyes. God, she's beautiful.

"I also like confetti cookies. They're my weakness."

"Really? I wish I knew that before I made pudding cups. I could have gone to Milk Bar and picked up some confetti cookies."

She shakes her head. "No, I adored your pudding cups and the added crushed-up Oreos and gummy worms. It was adorable."

"It was the only thing I could think of to make. My mom used to make them all the time when I was kid."

"I loved it." Her hand falls to my cheek. "You're very thoughtful, Wes. That's another thing I really like. And you listen. I know I sound unnecessarily critical of cell phones, but how often do you see couples out and instead of talking to each other, *listening* to each other, you see them playing with their phones? I like nights like this, and you don't seem to mind sitting here, listening to music, taking time to know me. My grandma once said that it's the true mark of a man worthy of me. *Time. Giving and receiving of time.* Clearly I forgot that with Doug." She pauses, and I want to tell her he was a major asshole for what he did to her. But I wait, because I think she knows that for herself now. "With you? I know from your touches and attention that you want me, but I've appreciated that you haven't seemed angered by my request to go slow. I fear you're ruining me for all other men."

"That's the goal." I laugh.

"Do you know what I've wondered though?"

"Hmm?" I ask, getting lost in her eyes.

"What your lips taste like. You seem to be so good at everything, so are you a good kisser too?"

Excitement shoots up my spine as my body practically shivers with desire. My hand falls to her thigh and I say, "Only one way to find out."

"I guess so." Her eyes fall to my lips as she asks, "You know, I've never had a guy kiss my ear before."

My head falls back on the couch. "Come on, I thought you were going to let that go."

She laughs and shifts her legs off my lap. I'm about to protest, until she straddles me and rests her hands on my chest. "How could I possibly let that slide? I need to add it to my running list of ways Wesley Waldorf Williams is human like the rest of us. Awkwardly kisses girls' ears. Wet kisses, actually."

"It wasn't that wet."

"It was pretty wet."

"It was average," I counter.

"Eh, above average." She curves her hands around my traps and whispers, "Want to kiss my ear again?"

"I hate you."

"No, you don't." She laughs and turns her head so her ear is right in line with my mouth. "Go ahead, I'm giving you free rein. Have at it. When you're done, give my earhole some tonguing to signal it's over."

Deadpanning, I say, "You think you're so funny, don't you?"

She faces me again. "I do. I really freaking—"

She squeals as I roll her onto the couch and move on top of her, trapping her under my body. Her eyes turn hungry and all joking is gone, as I lift my hand to her cheek and caress her soft skin with my thumb.

I lower my head, searching her eyes, looking for any indication she doesn't want this. But when her hand wraps around the back of my neck, I know I have the go-ahead.

I move my thumb over her bottom lip tracing the soft fullness of it, committing the feel to memory before lowering my mouth to hers. Millimeters away, I pause, and as she sucks in a harsh breath, I close the space, finally pressing my lips against hers. And fuck . . . fuck, it's so damn good.

Her lips work against mine, pressing into me, showing me she's just as hungry for this moment as I am, and that notion sends my stomach into a wild swirl of emotions.

She's greedy. It's a stark contrast to her outward calm, but her lips offer a different story, that this is exactly what she wanted to happen tonight. She was expecting it. Waiting for it.

With my thumb, I tilt her jaw up, giving me a better angle, and that's when I swipe my tongue across her mouth.

Once.

Twice.

And then she opens for me, her tongue greeting mine, matching each stroke. It's dizzying, heady, by far the best first kiss I've ever experienced. I'm not sure if it's because June herself is sending my entire body into a tailspin of lust, or if it's these deep-rooted feelings I'm starting to develop for her.

It's probably both.

Easily both.

Parting her lips more, she raises herself to match the fire I'm bringing, the heat that's swirling between us. So much heat I'm nervous that if I don't remove myself now, I'll take things too far, like slipping a hand up her short shirt, or making it clear how excited I am to be able to kiss her.

So with a final peck to her lips, I pull away and stare at her. Her eyes take a few seconds to open and when they do, I'm struck dead in the chest with her beauty, with the honesty that lies behind her pupils.

That was life-changing for her, just like it was for me.

When she catches her breath, she says, "And I like that. I like that a lot."

I smile down at her. "I like that a lot too, June."

"Then get back here," she says, pulling me down by my shirt, and I oblige, because I have a small amount of self-control left.

Only a little.

CHAPTER THIRTEEN

D*ear Modern Gentleman,*
      I introduced my girlfriend to my parents this past weekend and it was amazing. We had brunch at my parents' house, and we all sat around the dining table, exchanging stories and having one of the best times I've had in a long time. At one point my mom took my girl up to her room—my mom sells beauty products—and when they came back downstairs, my mom had given my girlfriend a makeover . . . or should I say, make-under. Awful, man, she looked awful, and the worst thing is, since then, she's continued to fluff her hair and wear her makeup just like my mom. It's disturbing how much they resemble each other, and I have no idea what to say because my girl is already self-conscious. How do I break it to her that the "improvements" are actually downgrades?
      Don't Want to Eff My Mom

                              Dear Don't Want to Eff My Mom,
First of all, right there with you. If my girl was sporting the same hair and makeup as my mom, we'd have a real issue. You want to be sensitive to your girl, especially if she has image issues already. So I would maybe gently tell her that even though you always think she's beautiful, she's showing a deep resemblance to your mom, and it's freaking you out. I'm sure if you throw

*down the gauntlet of not wanting to look down at her while you're
thrusting and picture your mom, that would snap her into shape. Give it a
shot and be as gentle as possible, and when she takes the shit off her face, go
alpha on that ass. Show her just how beautiful she is.*

Good luck, Gent,
The Modern Gentleman

WES

THE MEET AND GREET

"The time has come," I say once our drinks are delivered to our table.

Caden looks at me confused. "The time has come for what?"

I fold my hands on the table and look between my two friends. "The time has come for you two to meet June."

Roman leans back in his chair and twists his beer on the table. "You want us to meet your girl? Are you sure about that?"

"No," I answer on a laugh. "But I know things are getting serious. I met General Fitzbum's owner the other day, and June referred to me as her boyfriend. When we were walking through the park, I called her out on it and she shrugged casually and said, 'Yeah, you're my boyfriend.'"

"So it's official," Caden says. "Congratulations, man." He shakes his head. "Never thought this assignment would lead to you meeting someone. It's kind of crazy."

"Yeah, I think about that all the time. I wonder if I would have been as open to June if I hadn't felt pressured to find someone. I would have thought she was beautiful, but I don't think I would have asked for her phone number—"

"A phone number you didn't get," Roman points out.

"Either way. I'm not sure I'd have tried to ask for it if it wasn't for the assignment. Think I lucked out."

"How is the assignment going, by the way? Any news from Frank about the book thing?" Caden asks.

I shake my head. "Not yet. I turned in a proposal last week. Still think it's weird. Not sure anyone would want to read it, but whatever. If they want to publish it, that's fine with me."

"I bet they take it," Caden says. "It's a good gimmick. There could be a ton of sponsorships available, everything that would turn the regular guy into The Modern Gentleman. You could have your own clothing line, hygiene line, shoe line . . ."

"Lingerie line," Roman adds. "Dude, we could capitalize on this. I have experience in marketing, you know. Caden wants to be a CEO or COO of something. I say we break off from HYPE and create our own company."

"Uh, are you two insane? The only reason this is a possibility is because of Frank."

"Yes, but the intellectual property of The Modern Gentleman belongs to you. Frank can do all he wants, but you don't need to take anything from him. You could shop this proposal out to all publishers, not just his friend," Caden says.

Huh, do I really have intellectual property?

"I don't know. Feels like I'm going behind Frank's back."

"No, you're creating opportunities," Roman says. "Think about it, and before you sign anything, speak with us. Frank is most likely going to take credit and a percentage of all your hard work. You don't need him. He needs you."

"Without HYPE, The Modern Gentleman wouldn't be anything."

Caden takes a sip of his drink and says, "Without The Modern Gentleman, HYPE would have some serious financial issues. Look at the numbers, man. Your column is what brings readers to HYPE. Easily the most views on the entire website."

"We could create a successful brand," Roman says.

I look between my two best friends, confused how we got so off track.

"Maybe we table that idea right now and go back to why I brought you here: meeting June."

"What about it?" Roman asks. "You know we're going to meet her. Just tell us when and where."

"That's not it." I look them both in the eyes. "I don't want you embarrassing me."

They exchange looks and then laugh. "Okay, sure." Roman nods. "Yup, we won't embarrass you."

"I'm serious."

"Yeah, we know," Caden says with a smirk.

"Guys . . . please."

"We won't," they both say at the same time, and can you blame me? I don't believe them one bit.

"Before we go in there, I just want to remind you: take what they say with a grain of salt."

June smiles at me, cups my cheek, then stands on her toes, pressing a kiss to my lips. That will never get old.

Never.

"Don't worry. I can handle myself."

"You are not what I'm worried about," I say under my breath as I hold the door open for my girl. When she walks through, I slide my hand down her back to right above her ass and keep it there as I speak to the hostess. "Reservation under Williams."

"Ah yes, the rest of your party is already here, right this way."

Hand still on her lower back, I walk possessively next to June, spotting the guys in the back corner. When they see us, I carefully watch both of their reactions. Caden's brows both go up while Roman gives her a slow once-over.

Not surprised.

Ae we approach, they both stand. I quickly thank the hostess and then provide introductions. "June, this is Roman and Caden, my best friends. Guys, this is June, my girlfriend. Please don't be assholes."

"Never," says Roman, stepping up and pulling June into a hug.

Since Caden is in the corner, he gives her a handshake over the table, and then we all sit down.

"So, did I just get further with you than Wes after three dates?"

Pretty much.

June laughs and says, "I don't think we hugged until the third date, so that's accurate. Looks like you've been talking about me."

"More like blabbing, the guy won't stop talking about you. And we must applaud you," Roman says for both him and Caden. "You did quite the job on our man's balls. A-plus work. Top of the line. Never seen anything like it."

If this is a precursor to the night, I'm in for a long, long dinner.

"It was my first time using a tang to puncture someone's thang." She fluffs her hair. "But I think I nailed it."

Roman and Caden both break out in laughter while June moves her hand to my thigh, keeping it there for reassurance.

Okay, if she has to poke fun at me to get in with my boys, I'll allow it. I want them to get along—badly. I don't have family here, so these guys are like a pseudo-family to me. Their opinions matter.

"Did Wes tell you he dropped his pants so we could see the massacre you created at work? And our boss walked in, then screamed 'balls' down the hallway as he ran away?" Roman asks.

"Seriously?" June laughs and turns to me. "You showed these men your balls, even though I haven't seen them yet?"

"Uh, you just let me touch your leg for the first time the other day. Why on earth would I show you my balls? Especially under those conditions?"

"For the record"—she holds her finger up, and I'm loving the playful banter in her voice already—"you've been touching my leg for weeks now. Way to lie to look better in front of your friends." Both guys cover their mouths and say "ohhh" at the same time. "And also, I would've wanted to see your scrotum contusion because it's one of those things that you need to see, but don't want to see, but you can't look away . . . only to sprint away, as vomit climbs up your throat."

"It's the only reason I wanted to see it," Caden said. "And when I blink, sometimes I still see it."

"Shut the hell up." I chuckle.

"I have dreams of the right nut, trying to suffocate me with its swollenness," Roman says as the waitress comes to our table.

We quickly order drinks and dinner, and I'm grateful for the interruption, because once she leaves, Caden asks, "How are rehearsals, June? Wes told us you were cast in the chorus line for the revival of *The Music Man*. That's pretty incredible. The odds of being cast on a Broadway production are next to impossible."

"Thank you." June smiles brightly and squeezes my leg. "Rehearsals are great. Tiring, but great. I've never danced so much in my life and 'Seventy-Six Trombones' is on constant replay in my head, even when I sleep, but I'm having so much fun. I do miss my scheduled walks with General Fitzbum. I get to see him on the weekends, though, which is nice. But if you ever want to hear some gossip, hang around a Broadway chorus line. The things these people know—it's incredible."

"Like what?" Roman asks.

Our drinks are dropped off at the table and I take a sip of mine.

June says, "Dating within different companies is borderline incestual. Pretty sure everyone's junk has touched everyone's junk at this point. Besides me." She smiles over her shoulder. "And the drama, oh my God. This guy is cheating on that guy, but he's also seeing a girl, but then the guy was caught with the director as well? It's confusing but fascinating."

"I wouldn't mind stretching and lending an ear to whatever they have to say," Roman says.

"Oh, speaking of ears." June laughs. "They were talking about this advice column the other day and how some guy gave his date a wet willy." All three of us still. One thing I told the boys not to mention during our get together with June was The Modern Gentleman. I made them promise, especially since Frank put my job on the line if June found out. So the fact that she's talking about it now has me on high alert.

I eye Roman.

Roman eyes me.

Caden sips his drink.

I silently tell Caden and his conscience, *Don't say a goddamn thing.*

He replies with a clenched jaw. *I won't.*

Roman sniffs heavily. We both turn to him. *Do I get a warning?*

Say anything and die, I reply.

Jesus, settle down. Roman twists his drink on the table.

I really think he means murder. Caden shifts in his seat.

Murder by feral cats, I reply, eyeing both of them.

Well . . . at least in my head that's how it goes.

"Uh, did you tell them?" June asks, waving her hand in front of my face.

"Huh, what?" I ask, sweat creeping around my neck. Shit, I wasn't paying attention.

She glances around the table, taking in our guilty faces. June is incredibly perceptive, and I doubt she's going to let this moment pass.

When she folds her arms, eyeing us all, I know she's not going to.

"Were you three having a silent conversation without me?"

"No," I say while Roman nods.

"Yup."

Caden just stares at his drink.

"I see." She continues to scan the table. "And what exactly were you silently conversing about?"

My mind short-fuses, and I completely draw a blank. What were we talking about?

Well . . . death by feral cats, but that might have just been me.

"Approval, what else?" Roman says with a smirk. "A sly wink, a knowing nod. We approve, June."

Roman with the save. Which only means I'll owe him again.

She brings her hand to her heart and says, "Approval already? Man, that wasn't hard at all. I didn't even finish the story about how our first kiss was Wes kissing my ear. If anything, I knew that was going to win me approval."

"Come again," Caden says, leaning forward, most likely relieved to move past The Modern Gentleman thing.

"That's what I was getting to before you three started looking at each other weird." Okay, I feel guilty. "The wet-willy story reminded me of my first kiss with Wes and how he missed my lips completely and caught my ear."

"Because you turned your head." I laugh. "Not because I was aiming for your ear."

"Nonetheless, you kissed my ear."

Roman and Caden both laugh again, and even though I know our secret conversation *wasn't* about approval, I can see it in their eyes. They approve.

And that right there makes me one of the happiest guys there is.

～

"Want to come up?" June asks, holding my hand and tugging it toward her apartment complex.

"Yeah . . . I do," I say, unable to stop the huge smile that crosses my face.

"I thought you'd say that."

The first time seeing June's apartment. This could be one of the final hurdles to see if the girl is the real deal or not. A home tells a lot about a person. Right off the bat, just by their possessions, you'll know if they're a freak or not. Yeah, it's like judging a book by its cover, but if you get into a girl's apartment and she has a framed picture of Adolf Hitler hanging over her couch, you're going to think twice about asking her out again.

And yes, I realize I probably should have seen her apartment way before we gave each other the titles of "boyfriend" and "girlfriend," but of course, June has thrown my entire dating timeline out the window, and we've gone at her pace, something I've included in my articles—not relying on the provided timeline, but creating your own. What I'm offering is a basic outline. It's not concrete by any means. At least, that's what I've come to find with June.

Once we make it to her second-floor apartment, she unlocks the door and opens it. It's dark, so she holds my hand and guides me down the narrow hallway, where she flips the lights on.

"Holy mother of God," I nearly scream, backing into the wall behind me.

"Oh, sorry," June says, laughing as at least half a dozen dolls stare at us.

Lined up like an army platoon, each ringlet-headed doll has their right arm raised shoulder height and their head cocked to the side, eyes unblinking.

"I forgot to clean up my photo shoot before I left for our date. Completely forgot."

Hand to heart, I ask, "Why are they lined up like that? Staring, just . . . staring, waiting for when they're told they can blink?"

"Shows off the clothing at all angles." June bends down and scoops up the dolls, only to plop them into a box without care. "There, that better?"

"Do they . . . do they have names?"

"If they did, would you leave right now?"

"Good chance I might."

She chuckles. "Then nope, no names at all." She tugs on my

hand. "Come on, they're my mannequins. It's not like I set up tea parties with them on the weekends, complimenting the chapeaus they decided to wear to the mid-morning soiree."

"I sure as hell hope not."

She pulls me down on her couch and straddles my lap. "Would it help you forget about the dolls if we made out?"

"I mean, that would ease my anxiety." I glance around the rest of her apartment, everything else seeming normal and very June-like, with bright colors and her flare for the theater. "As long as they don't come alive and tap on my leg for a glass of water, I think we're going to be okay."

Calling out to the box of dolls, June says, "Did you hear that, Darla? Don't drag your limp doll leg over here for a glass of water. We're not interested in serving you tonight."

I still, my hands on her hips unmoving, my breath in my chest shortened, only for June to toss her head back and laugh, a throaty, full-of-life laugh.

"Oh God, your face just now was priceless." She shakes her head. "I promise, they don't move. They're as stiff as your erection the other night when we were making out."

I chuckle. "Yeah, not sure we're going to see maximum stiffness tonight."

June lightly caresses the side of my face and asks, "Are you scared of baby dolls, Wesley?"

"I'm scared of turning the lights on to see them all marching together, staring back at me with one thought in their eyes . . . murder."

"That wasn't the best introduction to my apartment, I admit, but I swear it's very comfortable here." She shakes my shoulders. "Relax. Have some fun." She moves my hands to her sides and guides them up. "After gaining approval from the best friends, I think we should get to know each other some more, don't you?" She moves one of my hands briefly across her breast and I swear I swallow my own tongue. "Aren't you curious what second base is like?"

More curious about a homerun, but I'll take second if she's handing it out.

"You know I am," I say, taking a deep breath, letting her move my hand around her body until she brings it back to her thighs and slips it under the hem of her dress. My head falls back on the couch and my gaze lands on her brilliantly greedy eyes as she moves my hand farther up until I reach her hip and the small piece of fabric wrapped around it. "Hell, June. What do you want? Tell me, and I'll give you whatever you want."

"Oh, I like the sound of that," she says, releasing my hand and leaning down to press the lightest of kisses across my mouth while she toys with the hem of my sweater, lifting if up, exposing my skin to the cool night air.

Did she mean second base with me . . . or with her? Clearly, I'd prefer with her, but if she wants to play around with my chest, flick around my nipples a bit, I guess there's nothing wrong with that.

As she continues to drag my sweater up, I hold her still, feeling my body relax and my dick harden. I know he won't get any action tonight, well aware of how slow this is going to be, but I make a promise to take care of things later. And by now, he knows I live up to that promise, because let's just say I've been more . . . handsy since my first kiss with June. Right now, I need to commit all this to memory, though. Every single silky second.

The feel of her sitting on my lap, her legs tightly clinging to each side of me.

The way her breath sounds shallow, turned on, with every pass of her hand over my bare skin.

The sound of her voice when she speaks softly, asking for what she wants.

"Lift up," she says. "I want your shirt off."

Excitement beats through me. Yeah, I can take this slow, as long as she keeps moving us forward, and this is the right direction. If I'm lucky, she might add some dry-humping into the mix. I shift forward on her slightly lumpy couch, she frees me of my shirt, and I lean back just as her eyes fall to my defined chest.

And the most horrifying sound of my life rings through her apartment.

As if Satan himself tickled his pointy Jafar-like fingers up my neck, and spoke directly into my ear, a demonic, gargled, and deathly deep, "MaMaaa," sounds through the apartment.

"Jesus, fuck," I say, scrambling up and off the couch, June tossed to the side. "What the hell is that?"

"Mama," the sound comes again, this time, slower, like it's dying. "Ma . . . ma."

"June, what the actual fuck?"

When I glance at her, she has tears running down her face, as she silently laughs and reaches into the crevice of the couch . . . pulling a naked doll out by the leg. The thing is missing an eye, its hair—the hair that's left—is reaching up to heaven, looking for salvation, and its nipples are green.

Why . . . why are the nipples green?

"Ma . . . maaaaa," it repeats in such a low voice, that I'm pretty sure it could beat out James Earl Jones for deepest voice over.

"Oh my . . . God," June says, while gripping her stomach and laughing so hard she bends at the waist and starts coughing. She wipes under her eyes, snagging her tears of humor. "I forgot Magdalene was in there."

"What the fuck is a Magdalene?"

"That's her name."

"Nope." I shake my head. "No, sorry. Can't do this." I reach for my shirt, and June laughs some more. She stands to stop me from dressing.

"Wes, stop. It's fine."

"Uh, did you hear the way that thing called out to you? It was like, if you didn't pop its eye back in its socket, it was going to start mapping out a plan to eat your foot while you're sleeping."

"It's an old doll—"

"It needs to go into the incinerator."

"No, she has the perfect measurements for a particular doll

that's quite popular with my older demographic. There's no way I'd ever get rid of her. Granted, bad timing to forget that she's stuck in the couch, but she's quite a lovely doll."

"Um, Margarine is anything but lovely."

"Magdalene," she corrects me.

"Either way, she's a nightmare." I drag my hand over my beard and say, "I really want to make out with you and let your hands wander, but I'm pretty sure my dick has turned inside out at this point."

"Oh God." She snorts and covers her mouth. "Really not a doll fan, huh?"

"No. Frankly, it speaks volumes right now that I'm still here in your apartment, talking rationally with you, instead of there being a Wes-shaped hole in your front door. Just goes to show how much I like you."

"Aww." She tosses the demonic doll into the box, it shouts off one more "mama," muffled and almost sad.

Good God, I will never be the same.

I'm shaken to my core—and yeah, maybe that's dramatic, but seriously, that thing could have dragged its plastic doll nails across my skin. Who knows what kind of diseases I could contract? And the nightmares I'll have, the thoughts of it popping out of nowhere in my apartment. I'm sleeping with a Swiss army knife in hand.

June helps me put my sweater back on. "I guess I'm oddly flattered that after such unprecedented encounters, you've been able to keep your wits about you—somewhat—and see through this evening."

"Frankly, it's a miracle."

Her hands fall to my chest. She lifts up on her toes and presses a quick kiss to my lips. "I'm sorry your penis shriveled up."

"Can't hear that enough from my girlfriend."

She chuckles and presses another kiss to my lips. "So I'm still your girlfriend despite you getting a glimpse of my freak flag?"

I slip my arm around her waist and keep her close. "Yeah, as long as those things are always put away when I come over."

"That can be arranged." She plays with the fabric of my shirt and says, "Thank you for introducing me to your friends tonight. I had a lot of fun with them."

"No need to thank me. I'm glad you met them, June July."

CHAPTER FOURTEEN

D*ear Modern Gentleman,*
        *Let's talk lingerie. Do I buy it for my girl? And if I do, what do
I get? I have some fantasies that I'd love to see her act out, but I'm nervous
she's going to see me waving my freak flag, lingerie attached to the top.
What are the dos and don'ts when it comes to buying intimate apparel for
my girl? I don't want to mess this up. Thanks.*
        Ready to Get Freaky

*Dear Ready to Get Freaky,
Lingerie, every man's fantasy, especially when the wearer struts into the
room, wearing nothing but a thong, bra, and thigh-highs on. That's
perfection right there. Your purchase really depends on how adventurous
your girl is and what she already has in her drawer. If she's the kind of girl
who keeps to the cotton affair, honor the fact that she likes to be comfortable.
Don't buy her a G-string and nipple tassels thinking that's going to work.
Keep it simple, classy. But if your girl is already spunky in that sacred
underwear drawer, I'd say push a little further past what she normally
wears, feel her out. If you get a green light, then I'd start seeing how much
further you can take it. Baby steps, though. And never, ever forget to tell her*

how sexy she is. The more confidence you can instill in her, the more you're going to be able to explore.

Good luck, Gent,
The Modern Gentleman

WES

THE DIRTY DEED

"How does your ass feel?" Roman asks, tossing me the basketball. We're casually shooting around, nothing serious, just getting out for some fresh air after five hours of meetings today.

Frank decided to have a brainstorming meeting going over all the analytics of each article, reading the comments, and seeing where we can make tweaks and adjustments.

Hell on earth is the only way to describe what we just went through, and the only thing that kept me from knocking myself out on the conference table was the spread of deli sandwiches and pickles brought in at one o'clock. It was a lifeline that pushed me through the end of the meeting.

Another reason I'm out here casually playing basketball is to help burn some of the excessive calories I consumed by eating four sandwiches.

Yes, four.

FOUR!

And three pickles.

Two cookies.

Three bags of chips.

#NotAshamed

There was nothing gentlemanly about my consumption of food today. Nope. I licked my fingers, I burped into my closed fist, and I sat back in my chair at one point and rubbed my stomach.

So why Roman is asking about my ass, I have no clue. If anything, he should see if I have any room left in my stomach.

"What are you talking about?" I ask, tossing up the ball and missing horribly to the left. Yikes, maybe Roman was right—my jump shot has suffered.

Caden picks up the rebound, bounces it into the basket, and then tosses the ball to Roman, who positions himself at the three-point line. "I just figured you might be sore after that meeting, you know, since Frank was crawling up your ass every chance he got."

Oh.

He's such an idiot—Roman that is, not Frank.

Well, Frank is an idiot too.

"I normally stay out of this shit," Caden says, stepping in. "But I agree, Frank was really up your ass today, and do you know why? Because he knows how valuable you are."

"Funny you say that, since he said anyone could take my place. Anyone could run the column."

"He said that because he's scared," Roman says, taking the shot and making it cleanly. "He's scared you're going to go off on your own. He might have good intentions with the whole book deal thing, but the numbers your column is pulling in surpass everyone's by the day. Especially with the new article. It's like reading a romance novel, but only getting a chapter every other day. People are chomping at the tit to find out what's going to happen next."

"The saying is 'chomping at the bit,'" I correct him.

"Not in my world. Always chomping at the tit over here." He winks and then steals the ball from me, knocking it out of my hands. "Face it, this thing exploded more than anyone expected. They talked about it on New York One this morning. It's only a matter of time before it goes to national TV."

"Which, in that case . . ." Caden gives me a look. I know that look. The morality police is clocking in. "You should really tell June what's going on."

"But Frank said—"

"That he'll fire you?" Caden rolls his eyes. "I dare him to. He would lose everything. The contract you signed when you came to HYPE clearly states you own the intellectual property. Did you not read it?"

Maybe not. *Winces*

"You might be full-time but you're also freelance in a way, bringing your idea and selling it on HYPE's website," Caden continues. "Frank can't do anything that would hurt you, which means you should tell June, especially since she's clearly hanging out with people who follow the article."

Information that could have been helpful earlier on . . .

"But I don't use names in the articles," I say, trying to wrap my head around all of this.

"So you're telling me if June read the articles you've written, she won't recognize that it's her?" Caden tosses the ball to me. "How many guys do you think get a contusion to the testicle on first dates?"

Valid point.

I toss the ball to Roman, who dribbles casually and then shoots and scores. "Hell, you might be right."

"I know I'm right. You need to tell her, and honestly, how would Frank really know? It's not like he can contact June. You're almost done with the assignment, your book proposal is done. You owe it to her to tell her, before this blows up even more, because from the looks of it, it's going to be huge."

"Yeah." I push my hand through my hair, thinking about the stats Frank put up on the screen today. They are alarmingly high. It actually made me sick to my stomach to see how many people are invested in my "How-To Guide." And I've been lucky. June is disconnected from that part of the world, thankfully, but I can't skate away without her knowing forever.

What will she say when I tell her, though? Will she believe I like her? That this isn't about tricking her for an article, but about me finding someone special?

"Why do you have that unsure look on your face?" Roman asks, holding the basketball at his side. "It's pretty simple, you just tell her."

"Yeah, but what if it doesn't go over well? What if she breaks up with me?" I run my hand through my hair. "I'm, uh . . ." I look off to the side. "I'm starting to fall for her."

"Starting?" Roman scoffs. "Dude, you're already plummeting off the cliff where this girl is concerned."

I don't want to admit it, but he's right. Things have moved pretty fast with June where my feelings are concerned. I think about her constantly, wishing I could text her throughout the day, waiting for the moment when I leave work and she's out of rehearsal and I get to see her, or just talk to her on the phone. Starting to fall for her seems like an understatement. I'm more than falling for her. I'm already there.

I feel it deep in my bones.

This girl was made to make me smile.

She was brought into my life to challenge me.

Our paths crossed so I could fall in love . . . for the first time in my life.

"Fuck," I mutter, putting both my hands on my hips.

"Yup, fuck is right," Caden says, patting me on the back. "Sooner rather than later, buddy. Rip the Band-Aid off. Trust us, you're going to be grateful you did."

❧

"Oh my God, you smell amazing," June says, flinging herself at me as she comes into my apartment. She runs her nose along my neck and takes a deep whiff, making me laugh out loud. "Seriously, that Man Soap is my undoing."

I shut the door behind her and wrap my arms around her waist, bringing her in for a kiss. "I missed you," I whisper against her lips.

"I missed you too. Three days is far too long to not see your handsome face." She practically climbs me like a tree, wrapping her legs around my waist. "And these lips. I missed them." Her mouth passes over mine, the pressure so light that it makes me dizzy more than anything. "Let's go to your bedroom."

I pull away. "Seriously?"

She chuckles. "To talk, hang out. Honestly, do you always have sex on the brain?"

"Yes," I deadpan. "Yes, June, I do. Especially when my girlfriend is as fine as you."

She chuckles and then hops down. That's when I take her in. Leggings, same cropped sweater she's worn before, hair tousled over her shoulders, still damp from her shower. Her rehearsals have been brutal lately, especially since they're closing in on opening day. Just a few more weeks and I get to see my girl on Broadway. There's nothing that can stop me from seeing her perform.

Hand in mine, she pulls me toward my bedroom but stops at the start of my hallway. Spinning around, excitement on her face, she says, "I almost forgot to tell you the big news."

"What?" I ask.

Purse still on her shoulder, she reaches into it and pulls out a phone, covered in a red case. "I bought a cell phone today."

"Are you fucking serious?" I ask, my eyes nearly falling out of their sockets.

"Yup, and guess whose number I put in first?"

"Better be mine," I say, pulling her in close and kissing the side of her head. "Does this mean I get to text you during the day?"

She nods. "Yes, and your first text better be a picture of us since I don't have any. I need something for my wallpaper."

I take my phone from my pocket and quickly unlock it. I have her enter her new phone number—she had to look at the settings to remember it—and then I send her every pic I have in my phone of us. We head into my room where we lie on the bed and look through the pictures, going over which one she thinks would be best. She doesn't want to use the same one I have, so she goes with a simple one of us in the park with the general.

"I can't believe you have a phone," I say as we both set our phones on the nightstand. "What made you get one?"

"Well, it's not because I was missing you more." She smiles as we face each other, my hand on her side, both her hands tucked under her head.

"Are you sure about that?"

"Well, maybe a bit more of that, but also my director made me get one. He said it was impossible to be informed of schedule changes without a cell phone, and I was burning through my pay-by-the-minute phone, so I caved. I spent two hours in the store this afternoon during my break getting the clerk guy to show me how to use it."

"I could have showed you."

She shakes her head. "No, I didn't want to have our heads buried in a phone when I came over. I haven't seen you for three days, and I wanted to look at your handsome face."

And that's just one of the reasons I've fallen for this girl. She's present. She's always present with me.

"That's a good answer, June July."

"It's the truth." She twists our legs together and says, "So what have I missed in the last few days?"

This would be the perfect time to tell her about the article, the assignment, and the book proposal, but as I stare into her smiling eyes, taking in the way they sparkle when they look back at me, I don't want to break this moment. I haven't seen her in three days, I've missed her terribly, and all I want to do is get wrapped up in her, just for the evening.

Swallowing hard, I draw a circle on her bare side and say, "Not much, just me pining after my girl, waiting for her to call me when she got home."

Propping her head up, she asks, "Have you been pathetic, Wes?"

I chuckle and nod. "Really pathetic."

"Poor guy." She reaches out and pats my cheek. "What did you miss?"

"Everything," I sigh. I move my hand to her ribs, loving her silky soft bare skin under my palm. "Your smile, your teasing, the way you so easily bust my balls, and your compliments. I love that you say whatever you want." I slide my hand under her cropped sweater, and her eyes turn to fire. "And I love the way you look at me, with passion, intrigue, and intensity. No one has ever looked at me the way you do." I move my hand up farther and she sucks in a breath . . . and that's when I realize she's missing something. She bites on her bottom lip as I barely croak out, "Are you not wearing a bra?"

She shakes her head. "Thought it would be easier to get to second base."

"Christ," I say, moving in closer and moving my hand to right below her breasts. As if she just soaked my body in gasoline and flicked a lit match on me, my entire body is encased in flames as our foreheads press together.

Removing one hand from under her head, she smooths it down my shirt, under my hem, and then back up my stomach. "I've thought about you every day, feels like every second of every day," June says, her fingers playing with the divots of my abs. "I've thought about what it would feel like to have your hands all over me, your lips traveling over every last inch of my body, to hear the sounds you make when my hand roams . . ." She travels up to my chest, her fingers running over the pad of my nipple.

I hiss out a sharp breath. "June," I say on a sigh, looking into her eyes. She moves in closer, causing my hand to skim the bottom of my breast. Fuck.

"Touch me," she whispers, her lips gliding over mine, but not fully connecting. "Feel me, Wes."

Body thrumming, need coursing through me like a tidal wave, my mouth descends on hers just as I move my hand up and over the soft globe of her breast and fuck, is it everything.

Soft and warm fills my palm with her pebbled nipple already taut and turned on.

So hot.

I groan into her mouth as she pushes her chest into my hand, her top leg wrapping around mine, pulling me in even closer.

I squeeze her breasts, dragging my thumb over her nipple, loving the way she wiggles beneath me, how she moans into my mouth. She continues to kiss me, even though little gasps of surprise pop out of my mouth every time I stroke or pinch her nipple differently.

Out of breath, she pulls her mouth away and her eyes search mine. I wish I could read her thoughts, know precisely what's going on in that pretty head of hers. Before I can decipher what she needs next, she sits up, pushes me to my back, and straddles my lap, only to lift her sweatshirt up and over her head, revealing two perfect breasts with aroused nipples.

"Fucking hell, June," I say, dragging my hand over my beard. She takes the hem of my shirt and lifts it up and over my head, baring me to her. I watch as she sighs in contentment and moves her hands over my stomach, up to my carved pecs.

"Your body isn't fair," she says. "I swear you're too good to be true."

"I think that about you every goddamn day," I say as she lowers her body, her breasts resting against my chest, her mouth connecting with mine. Instinctively, my hands go to her back where they travel the slope to her ass, where I slip one hand under the waistband of her leggings. Only a few inches, testing her responsiveness and willingness to progress things, and when she doesn't pull away, I keep my hand there.

And when her hips start to ride mine, all the blood in my body pools to my center, sending my cock into overdrive.

I move my mouth to her jawline, down her neck where I nibble on the column.

"No hickies," she says breathlessly. "Can't cover them up for rehearsal."

"What about on your tits?" I ask, traveling my mouth down as she lifts just slightly, giving me access.

"Do whatever you want to them."

If that's the case . . . I flip her to her back and bring my mouth to them where I suck one into my mouth while palming the other.

"God, yes, I knew you'd be good at this," she moans, her back arching.

I suck on her breasts for a good few minutes, listening to the soft sounds she makes, the way her body reacts to the different ways I play with them. Testing her, I move lower and kiss the underside of her right breast, then her ribs, then her stomach. I look up at her and watch her chest rise and fall more rapidly as I travel lower. When I reach her belly button, I ask, "June, can I taste you?"

"I couldn't stop you if I wanted to at this point."

That's one way to make my dick harder . . . giving me the green light.

Fingers in the waistband of her leggings and her underwear, I pull them down together and strip her completely naked. I don't move between her legs right away. Instead, I absorb the beautiful woman lying in front of me.

Slender shoulders, soft, turned-on breasts, firm stomach, narrow waist, round hips, toned legs, bare and beautiful.

"You're stunning," I whisper in awe, shocked that June is mine, and that I'm lucky enough to not only have her in my bed but have her in my life as well. I bring one of her legs up to my mouth and kiss the inside of her calf, her knee, her upper thigh. She sucks in a sharp breath when I grow close but then lower her leg and prop it up on the bed so her knee is bent, only to repeat the same thing with her other leg.

When I reach her center, I move my hand between her legs and part her bare skin only to lower my mouth to her aching center.

From the first contact of my tongue, her body shocks against the mattress, her hands gripping the comforter below us.

"Oh my God, Wes," she says on a heavy sigh.

From her reaction, I'd say she hasn't had this done in a while. Wanting her to remember this moment, I flick the tip of my tongue against her clit in short, rapid strokes, applying enough pressure to feel her body tighten under my hold.

"Yes, right there. Please don't move." She shifts, her head lifting to look at me, her stomach hollowing out. "How are you this good? How do you know . . . oh God." Her head falls back. "Wes, it's too fast. I don't want to come this fast."

I lift my tongue off her but keep her parted.

"No, don't stop," she says, making me laugh.

"You didn't want to come."

"I'm just shocked, please, don't stop. I was right there."

Chuckling a bit more, I peek my tongue out, but instead of the short flicks, I flatten my tongue and take long swipes up her center. Her hand falls to my hair and she grips tightly as her hips twist from side to side, her heels digging into my back.

"Oh . . . Jesus. Wes, yes, you're so good. You're so damn good." I move back to flicks, and her hips flex, one hand pulls on my hair, her other digs into the blankets. Her breasts peak, her stomach becomes shallow, her lips fall open and the most beautiful, feral cry calls out of her mouth as she comes on my tongue. Her pussy is so slick as I let her ride out her orgasm until she can't take it anymore.

While she lies there, catching her breath, I get rid of my pants and I reach into my nightstand for a condom. My cock is hard as stone, straining between my legs, looking for relief.

Detecting me above her, she opens her eyes to get an eyeful as I lean over her for the condom. Her hand immediately wraps around my cock and she pulls on it, using the precum to lubricate her hand.

"Shit," I huff as she moves her hand up and down my length.

"I want you in my mouth," she says. "Climb higher on the bed."

Condom still in my hand, I move so my bottom half is near her face and my hands rest on the headboard, and before I can get myself situated, she takes my cock in her mouth, causing my head to fall forward as she sucks hard on the tip.

"Holy fuck," I grind out while one of her hands moves up and down my length, the other gently gripping my balls. "Ah, June, that feels amazing."

She's tender with her hands, not stroking too hard, not gripping too tight, but her mouth is a direct contrast. Her suction is unreal, and the way her tongue swirls around the head of my cock is blurring my vision.

"I . . . want to . . ." I breathe out, squeezing my eyes shut when she flicks her tongue along the underside of my cock. "Come inside you," I rush out with a groan. God, fuck . . . that feels so good. So fucking good.

After a few more strokes, she pulls her mouth away and says, "Then come inside of me."

When June breaks the seal on something, she apparently goes all in, and right now, she's 100 percent full steam ahead, making this one of the best nights of my life.

Lowering my body away from her, I rip open the condom and sheath myself, keeping my eyes on June the entire time. She spreads her legs wider and reaches for me. I fall on top of her and cup her face, my thumb stroking her cheek, my cock pressed to her center. I lower my mouth to hers, crushing our lips together, the fury for this woman igniting an entirely new wave of heat through my body as I get closer and closer to her.

She lowers her hand to my cock and presses it against her entrance.

My tongue dives into her mouth.

Her hips rock forward.

I barely enter her.

"Fuck," I breathe out heavily, moving so I have a better angle to pump into her. One hand on either side of her shoulders, I feel my muscles tense as I push deeper and deeper inside until I bottom out. We both groan together from the connection, our mouths quickly finding each other, our needs soaring.

I fucking need every piece of this woman.

I need her mouth, her hands, her breath, the beat of her heart connecting with mine.

Every goddamn piece.

I flex my hips into her and her chest lifts, her mouth parting. I repeat the flex and every time I move inside her, her reaction becomes sexier.

Hands to my arms.

To my shoulders.

Her legs around my waist.

Her heels to my lower back.

Pressing.

Gripping.

Tightening.

Together we climb.

Our mouths collide, our tongues dance, our heat builds and builds to an unrelenting inferno.

The sensations around us mix together. Air turns into harsh breaths. Moans meld into a symphony. Thrusts become an erotic dance, working together. And hands become lifelines, the only thing keeping us from falling over as they cling, grip, anchor to anything to keep our minds afloat, our bodies holding on to this apex.

Holding on to this moment in time where gravity doesn't exist.

Where pleasure sears through our veins.

Where the only thing we see is each other. The only thing we feel is our connection and the pulsing beat of our orgasms, knocking down every last wall we've built until it crashes and explodes through us with one last thrust.

"Oh my fucking God," June shouts, her pussy clenching around me.

"Fuck . . . fuck me," I groan, my balls tightening as my cock swells quickly and then bursts with my come, filling the condom as I still above her, the muscles in my back contracting, the bones in my body bursting into shrapnel, making me feel lifeless and weak.

I fall onto the bed, my body half on hers, half on the mattress, my breath escaping from my lungs at a rapid rate.

Her hand smooths over my back as I feel our breaths start to mix together, filling our lungs deeply, bringing us back to earth.

That was . . . I can't fucking explain it. It was ungodly, unreal, unlike anything I've ever experienced and it's evident why, because when I lift up to prop my head on my hand and look down at my girl, I realize one thing.

I'm in love with this woman.

My love for her is strong.

Unrelenting love.

The kind of love that only comes once in a lifetime.

The kind of love I need to hold on to.

The kind of love that deserves honesty and truth.

Her hand lifts to my cheek. "Are you okay?" she asks, stroking my face with her thumb.

I swallow hard and nod. "Amazing. You're . . . amazing."

I desperately want to tell her how I feel about her, that she's changed my life in the best way possible, that she's all I think about, all I want. I want to tell her the truth about the assignment. I want to lay it all out, beg her to understand and hope she does.

But if there is one thing I tell my readers over and over again: post-coital moments aren't meant for confessions; they're meant to soak in the moment, to let the taste of each other sit on your tongue, to savor the connection you just made.

It's not the time to confess love.

It's not the time to talk about real life.

It's not the time to admit to an indiscretion.

Instead, you push those thoughts out of your mind, pin them for the next day, and love on your significant other. Snuggle, cling to them, let them know that nothing is more important than this moment between you both, and committing it to memory.

And that's exactly what I do.

I don't tell her. But, remember the collective, "Wes, you're an idiot?"

Well, I think we all know why . . .

So, that's why I end up drinking one of her lady drinks, broken-hearted, and listening to Joni Mitchell while Caden questions my sanity.

~

A nd there you have it, how it all went down.

How my life was flipped upside down by a girl, only for me to lose everything.

Sighs, grips lady can, clings to scarf

But if we break it down . . . did I really have a choice? Let's look at all the factors here: I was afraid of losing my job, I was—

HOLD UP.

Snaps fingers

Hey, you. Yeah, you. Reader. That's right, I'm talking to you. Look over here. *Waves*

Hi. June here, I think we need to flip this story for a second, because I'm over it.

Want the truth of how it went down instead of the runaround? Flip to the next page. I'll tell you exactly how your friend Wesley Waldorf messed this up.

CHAPTER FIFTEEN

D ear June July,
    Why is Wes such a dumbass?
Confused Reader

> Dear Confused Reader,
> Aren't all men dumbasses? Don't worry, I'm about to explain how it all
> went down and pinpoint exactly why he's a dumbass.
> Hang in there, you beautiful bibliophile.
> June July

JUNE

THE FUCK UP

A bout time I get a chance to speak. Sheesh. That boy sure knows how to blab on.

You would think given Wesley is supposedly The Modern Gentleman—yeah, I know who he is, we'll get to that in a second —he'd let me tell my point of view every other chapter, but nope, he decided to hog the spotlight for himself.

Should have known he wasn't really the gentleman he claimed to be.

Before we get into the specifics, I guess I should catch you up on the CliffsNotes of my life, huh?

I'll be quick, don't worry. I'm not looking to entertain you with fancy descriptions of orgasms here, like our friend Waldorf. Let's get to the facts. The nitty-gritty.

Met a handsome stranger in the park. Ungodly attractive.

Mr. Fancy Hair dropped into my life just like General Fitzbum dropped a doo-doo on the sidewalk. I'd never seen a man so put together, so dignified for his age. I knew there had to be something about him that wasn't right.

But the more I got to know him, the more I found out that he was just a nice guy—at least that's what I thought.

But honestly, how could I not at the time? The things he went through when dating me . . .

I clocked him in the testes, nearly punctured them, and he still wanted to see me.

I thought he was either a glutton for punishment, one of those red-room types, or he really liked me. Either way, I was down for both.

He was a fun drunk, love-thrusting his crotch.

He took a fire retardant to the face like a champ.

Smelled like a GD bearded pheromone every time I saw him.

And could take on any kind of tormenting joke I tossed in his direction, absorbing it like a sponge and clutching it like it was giving him life.

But what really won me over was when we went to a hibachi

grill, where he spilled his beer twice down his shirt, choked on a flying shrimp the chef tossed at him, which led to me giving him the Heimlich. When the check came, he realized he'd forgotten his wallet, resulting in him meeting his friend outside for cash, where he tripped on the sidewalk and fell into sewage water, and then proceeded to hold my hand and call me a cab, without breaking a sweat. Oh, he didn't tell you about that date?

Taps chin

I wonder why.

Maybe because I had to fling him around like a ragdoll, dislodging kung pao shrimp from his throat. Apparently, he was emasculated enough in the recounting of his other tales, he left that special diddy out.

But any man who could go through such a night and still hold his head high was a guy I could fall for.

Oh yeah. The big L for this girl.

Besides the fact that he is the hottest man I'd ever seen, the bearded wonder with lips to die for, he was sweet, interested, thoughtful, and truly got to know me.

I fell hard.

That night, when we finally had sex for the first time, it wasn't just sex to me. It was making love. Yeah, I might sound like an old-fashioned cornball right now, but it's true, I gave him my heart that night, only for him to tear it apart the next morning.

Curious?

Want to know how THE FUCK UP happened?

Prepare your hearts, because I'm about to pile on some General Fitzbum doo-doo to this story.

Let's circle back to the morning after mind-blowing orgasms, but from my point of view this time, if you don't mind.

Ahem

~

"Good morning," Wesley's deep morning voice says, as his lips press against my temple, his arms coming back around me after he shuts off his alarm. "You're so damn warm."

"What time is it?" I mutter, my eyes not wanting to cooperate with me just yet.

"Five thirty."

"Ew, why do you wake up that early?"

He chuckles into my ear, the rumbling sound falling over my skin, spreading goosebumps. "I have early meetings today with some advertisers and I need to prep for them." He kisses the spot below my ear. "Feel free to stay in bed. I'm hopping in the shower. I'd ask you to join me, but I know that's going to result in being late."

"It's too early to have a penis impale me," I say, draping my arm over my face.

"Not a morning-sex person. Got it." He kisses me one more time and starts to move away when he stops and rests his hand on my bare stomach, his thumb caressing my skin. "Hey, last night meant a lot to me. I hope you know that."

Ugh, see why he's perfect? What guy tells a girl that their first sexual experience meant a lot to them?

Usually it's a "Fuck, that was amazing."

Or a "That was so hot."

Maybe "You made my dick so wet last night," for the dirty talkers.

But "Last night meant a lot to me"? That's what you read in stories and watch in movies, that's not real life. At least it's not for other people.

It seems to be for Wes.

He leans down and presses a kiss to my forehead, his lips lingering, and even though I'm not a morning person, his words, his gentle caresses, they wake me up, turn my insides into goo, and cause me to swoon like a damsel in distress.

"It meant a lot to me too," I answer, because it did.

I love him.

So much.

He's so much more than I ever thought I could find in a man. He makes me laugh constantly. He shows great humility but never lets it cloud his judgment or ruin our time together. His attention to detail like walking next to the street when we're making our way through the city, his hand pressed to my lower back, or his thoughtfulness when it comes to the little things like where he takes me out on a date. His patience and understanding are greater than any I've ever experienced. And his ability to make me feel cherished is beyond compare.

I like him as a man.

Adore him as a friend.

Love him as mine.

Simple as that.

He smiles down at me and exhales. "You're giving me all kinds of feels, June." He kisses me one last time and then says, "Got to get in the shower."

"Hey, I forgot to ask you something last night."

"What's that?" he asks, his smile contagious.

"The company is getting together next Friday at Chuck's Diner for a pre-production dinner. We're allowed to bring a guest and since I know you play basketball some nights, I figured I'd try to get on your schedule early."

He chuckles and says, "June, I'd clear my schedule for you. Next Friday? It's a date." He plants one more kiss on my lips and then, naked as the day he was born, he hops out of bed. I watch his tight and firm backside walk into the bathroom, reminding me just how lucky I am.

He keeps the door to the bathroom partially open so the light filters into the room. I'm sure he doesn't do it on purpose, but with the light streaming in and the roar of emotions pulsing through me, there is no going back to sleep for me, so instead, I reach for my phone on his nightstand that he so sweetly charged for me last night.

When it comes to life, there are a few text messages from the chorus line text thread. I'm still getting used to all the craziness of having people be able to reach me at the tip of their fingers, so when I open the thread, I'm fairly overwhelmed.

I scroll to the start of the most recent from last night and see that it's from Charlie, one of the guys who is sleeping with the director.

Charlie: *Did anyone see yesterday's installment from The Modern Gentleman? I just about peed myself. [Link]*

Rebecca: *Oh my God, I know. The poor guy. I don't want to know what a contusion to the nutsac looks like.*

I pause, scrub my eyes.

Wait, what?

I sit up and rest my back against the bed, my muscles aching from last night's activities and rehearsals.

Patricia: *With a shuffleboard stick nonetheless. I almost threw up reading it.*

There's no way.

Kurt: *Wait, June, didn't you puncture your boyfriend the first time you went out? Sounds oddly familiar.*

Rebecca: *That's where I heard the story from. OMG, is your boyfriend The Modern Gentleman?*

What the hell is The Modern Gentleman?

Glancing toward the bathroom door, I hear him in the shower. Confused, tired, and not in the mood for any of this, I'm about to exit out of the text thread when I glance at the link again.

A contusion to the testicles by a shuffleboard tang. That is way too coincidental.

Wes is a writer for an online website. Could it be?

Before I can stop myself, I click on the link. Maybe he is The Modern Gentleman fella and he's putting himself out there about our first date. Kind of noble if you think about it, admitting to getting taken out by your date the first time you go out.

The article comes up and my eyes quickly fall to the source.

HYPE

Written by The Modern Gentleman. No picture, no second name. I glance over the title and see that the article is being written in "Episodes." Under the title is a quick blurb.

Our very own modern gentleman has set out onto the streets of New York to show all you gents out there that securing a girl isn't as hard as it seems. Follow his step-by-step outline in wooing, charming, and securing a girl The Modern Gentleman way through real-life examples. That's right, our modern gentleman is here to show you just how easy it is as he takes his practices to real life. Watch and learn, gents.

What?

I blink some more.

No, there is no way this is Wes. He wouldn't . . . do that, would he?

Use me as a test subject?

Not possible.

I look away, setting my phone on my lap. The water stops and I hear his shower door creak, as a wave of anxiety hits me.

I pick my phone back up and go to episode one, and when I read the title, my heart seizes in my chest.

We Met Over Dog Poop.

Subtitle: You read that right, dog poop, but see how I turn a crappy situation into a dating opportunity.

No.

No, this can't be happening.

I scan the article, unflattering tales of our walks fly through my head, the way he tackled each situation with The Modern Gentleman techniques. I skim through the rest of the episodes, my relationship with Wes unfolding in front of me, but told from a completely different perspective.

Clinical almost.

Scientific.

Follow these steps, get this result. See, it worked for me?

It's all been for an article, every last minute of it.

And what was last night?

How to finally get laid? What to say the next morning to make the girl fall head over heels for you?

All the things he's said to me feel calculated now. Weightless. Without substance.

A wave of nausea rolls through my stomach as I spring from the bed and quickly get dressed. I'm in the midst of gathering my things when Wes comes through the bathroom door, wearing nothing but a low-slung black towel around his waist.

"Hey, headed out so soon? I was going to make us some breakfast."

"Oh, is that so?" I ask, standing tall, pushing my hair out of my face. "What step in the process would that be?"

"What?" he asks, a crinkle to his brow.

"The Modern Gentleman process, Wes." His face falls, and that right there tells me everything I need to know.

"June, it's not what you think."

"Oh, I'm sure." I sardonically laugh and go to his entryway, where I find my shoes and quickly slip them on.

"June, wait, let me explain."

"I'm pretty sure I already know the answer, but I figure I should ask anyway." I turn to face him. "Are you The Modern Gentleman?"

He pulls on his wet hair, his bicep flexing tightly as he strains. "Yes," he answers, looking me straight in the eyes.

"Wow. Okay." I choke back the tears that want to fall, the emotion clogging my throat.

"But you have to understand, June, that's all a persona."

"Really? From what I briefly read, it seems like all the things you're telling your readers to do, your equation to scoring the girl, are the things you used on me."

"Yeah, that looks bad." He scratches the back of his neck. "But it was never an equation for me with you, June. Hell, you are such a wild card, you made me feel completely out of my element."

"So I wasn't the typical girl you usually fool with your charm? Well, I'm glad I could offer you a challenge this go-around."

"It wasn't like that," he says, growing frustrated.

"Okay, tell me this, did you or did you not ask me out because it was an assignment for your job?"

He winces. "At first, yes."

"And that's all I need to know." I grab my purse, and he quickly comes after me, grabbing my arm.

"June, please, I was going to tell you last night. I was, but then you—"

"Don't you dare blame your inadequacies of being an honest man on me. It is not my fault you apparently don't carry a conscience bone in your body, that's yours."

"My boss threatened to fire me," he says in panic. "I didn't tell you at first because I couldn't afford to be replaced."

"Ah, so your ethics are questionable as well. Good to know."

"June, don't leave, please just let me—"

"Explain?" I finish for him. "Don't bother. I have all the information I need from you." I shake my head. "I can't believe I fell for you." My voice catches in my throat and he takes a step forward, but I hold my hand out, stopping him. Looking him in the eye, I say, "I expected so much more from you, Wes. Then again, I guess I was expecting excellence from someone I guess I don't even know."

"That's not true." He presses his hand to his chest. "I'm the same person, June. Nothing has changed between us. Everything we experienced, it was real. It's all real."

"It was real to me, Wes. It was a project to you. I was only a project."

"That's where you're wrong. You weren't a project to me. Not even from the first moment I met you. You were never a project. You have to believe me, June."

"I don't have to do anything," I say, gripping the door to this apartment. "This is over, Wes. Maybe when you write your final episode, you can inform readers that being truthful and honest might have saved this relationship, that instead you chose to be a dumbass and hide it from me. Maybe you're not as smart as I thought you were."

"June, wait," he calls out as I open the door.

I pause, look over my shoulder and say, "Wes, please do us both a favor and crawl up your barely healed scrotum and drown in your sperm." His look of shock does nothing to make my broken heart feel remotely better. Before I leave, I say, "Don't try contacting me. I'm not going to answer."

With that, I flee his apartment, my heart in my throat, tears tickling my eyes, and a trail of embarrassment and regret following behind me.

How could I have been so stupid?

I'd thought going slow would keep my heart out of the equation. I'd thought the pace Wes accepted was because to him, I was worth the wait.

But no. Going slow gave him more fodder for his article.

For his experiment.

For his job.

I knew he was too good to be true.

I just knew it.

CHAPTER SIXTEEN

D ear Modern Gentleman,
      I messed up. Big time. Without getting into details, I totally blew it with my girl. I neglected to tell her something and she found out. It was stupid and I'm kicking myself in the ass for not being open and honest with her. I know that's what you harp about constantly. I'm at a loss. I love her and I need her back in my life, but I have no idea how to go about earning her trust again. Any suggestions?
      Dumbass

Dear Dumbass,
My suggestion to you: go back in time and make the right choice.
You're screwed.
Good luck, Gent,
The Modern Gentleman

WES

THE GROVEL

"There he is, the man of the hour. I have some good news—" Frank pauses in the door to my office. "What's, uh . . . what's going on here?" He bends at the knees slightly to take me in at a different angle. "Are you crying?"

Yup. I am.

I'm crying.

I'm crying like a goddamn baby and I can't seem to stop it.

The only thing that's different from yesterday to today? I'm showered, wearing a suit, and I ditched the scarf and lady drink. But I'm still very much a broken man inside.

And yes, I know, I did this to myself. I see the neon sign that says "dumbass," with an arrow pointing over my head. I'm well aware the mistakes I made are why I'm in this situation. I'm not looking for pity, I'm just telling it like it is.

My chest hurts.

My body aches.

My head feels like it's about to explode.

And all I want is to cuddle into my girl, smell her hair, and hold her boob.

Is that too much to ask?

A simple palm to breast to soothe my aching soul?

I wipe my eyes and move some papers around on my desk. "What's up, Frank?"

He doesn't step into my office, but instead stays in the doorway, gripping it with both hands, as if he's holding on, waiting for someone to dislodge him from the hell he unsuspectingly stepped into.

"Why are you crying?"

"Allergies," I sniffle, trying to get my mind to stop thinking about June and all the ways I won't be able to win her back. My eyes shift to the list on my desk, the pathetic list of ways to win her back, all of them pure crap, all of them real losers.

"That doesn't look like allergies."

"What do you want, Frank?" I snap at him.

He doesn't answer right away. He studies me, though, looking unsure and uncomfortable. I'm about to snap at him one more time when he says, "Um, my publisher friend said he's very interested in your book proposal."

"Cool," I say, keeping my head focused on my computer.

"Cool? That's all you have to say? Cool?" He steps into my office but shuts the door. "Can you explain to me why you're not more excited?" I don't answer. "Does this have to do with you crying?"

"I'm not . . . crying," I say, choking up and then wiping my eyes again.

Frank takes a seat, his purple velvet suit jacket boldly bright and reminding me of a dress June once wore, a dress that made her eyes stand out and her hair look like tempting fire.

More tears well in my eyes and the last thing I want to do is be the guy who's sobbing at work over a breakup. But . . .

Raises hand

I'm that guy.

Tears flood my eyes and my head falls to my desk as a sob rips through me.

Frank clears his throat. "Are you still going to claim allergies?"

"She . . . broke up with me," I say, getting all the words out before another sob.

"June?" Frank asks. "June broke up with you?" I nod against my desk. "Why?"

I look up, and a Post-It stays stuck to my forehead. I don't bother removing it; that's how pathetic I am. "Why do you think? She found out about the article."

"You never told her?"

"What?" I ask. "You told me not to."

"That was when you first started out. I didn't want you

plaguing the girl's mind with what we were doing, I wanted an authentic experience, but once you started developing feelings for her, you should have told her. What does The Modern Gentleman always say? Be open and honest."

You've got to be fucking kidding me.

"Frank, you threatened my job."

"To light a fire under your ass, and it worked. You were far too complacent in your position. Yes, you are the bread and butter of this website, we can all see that, but you were starting to fall into a rhythm that was running dry. You needed to be sparked again, and you were. But honestly, Wes, any gentleman would have known when things got serious that's when you have a conversation with your girl."

"I can't freaking believe this." I push away from my desk. "Frank, you can't threaten my job to get what you want."

"Yes, I can. I'm your boss. You were in a rut. If you continued in that rut, it would leave me with nothing else to do than replace you. I'm glad that's not the case here, but I treated you like any other employee who has become complacent in their job. I've seen your potential to branch out in the publishing world for quite some time now, start a brand, but how were you going to do that just going through the motions?"

"Wait, hold on a second. You want me to branch out?"

"Why wouldn't I? It would be best for both of us and you did bring the idea for the column to HYPE. I'd rather work with you than against you. I see you guest blogging with us, still running the column, but also working on a brand that ventures out to all things Modern Gentleman."

I can barely wrap my head around what he's saying, and how it matches everything Roman and Caden have said. Here I thought Frank was the bad guy when, in fact, he was looking out for my best interests.

Why does he have to be so . . . eccentric? So hard to read?

"I don't know what to say."

"Well, the business side of things we can focus on later, because it seems like we have to deal with more pressing matters. How do we get June back? What are your ideas?"

Am I really doing this? Plotting with Frank?

From the way he gets comfortable in the chair across from me, I'm guessing yes.

"Get on with it, we don't want much time to pass," he encourages.

Clearing my throat and wiping my eyes again, I pick up my sad piece of paper and read through it.

"These are just ideas, but uh . . . send flowers."

"Oh boy." Frank brings his hand over his eyes and massages his head. "I can see that maybe your powers of being The Modern Gentleman are diminished by the fact that you're grief-stricken right now, which is understandable, so why don't I lend a hand?" He folds his hands and asks, "Have you apologized?"

I think back to our fight. "Uh, I don't think I got the chance to."

"Okay, well that's job number one." He points to my paper. "Write that down." I quickly jot down notes. "Now, we need to make a grand gesture, something that you've talked to her about on one of your dates, something that will prove—"

A light bulb goes off in my head. "I have just the thing."

"That's the ticket," Frank claps his hands. "Now tell me all about it."

~

Wes: *Before you get mad at me, I want you to know, I tried incredibly hard to crawl up my own testicle and drown in my unborn children, but despite valiant efforts, it was next to impossible. Which leads me to texting you. And before you tell me to eat crap and die, I want to tell you this . . .*

Wes: *(Started a new text message for effect)*

Wes: *(Did you get dramatic pause? Doesn't matter, I'll proceed.)*

Wes: *I'm sorry, June. I should have told you everything. I was stupid* *and scared, and honestly, didn't think you would see the article, given your non-existent penchant for technology.*

Wes: *But that's not an excuse. I should have practiced what I preach and been honest with you. I was nervous about what you would have said. I was nervous to lose you, but I guess I already have.*

Wes: *I know you're at rehearsal right now, but I want you to know I miss you and I'd love to talk with you. To make this right.*

June: *What a great apology. But can I ask you something?*

Wes: *Yes, of course, anything.*

June: *Did you try waterboarding yourself with your own sperm?*

Wes: *I'll uh . . . I'll try that next.*

June: *Perfect.*

~

"June, hey, June." Not even bothering to stop, she passes right by our tree and continues on her walk with the general. I know on Tuesdays June uses her lunch break to walk the general. I was hoping she was going to take the usual route and when I saw her appear, I was shocked but also relieved.

But now that I'm chasing after her, it feels weird.

"June. Hey, June. Hold up." I sprint after her thanks to her intense power-walking. General Fitzbum has extra pep in his step. Jesus.

When I finally catch up and step in front of her, I spot her with a whistle in her mouth.

"Hey, what, uh, what's that?"

She takes it out of her mouth for a brief second. "A rape whistle."

"If you're scared, I can walk—"

She blows it, giving it two loud toots.

What the hell?

She nods at me, blows it again and . . .

Oh shit.

I hold my hands up and back away. "Got it, okay." I step aside and let them walk by.

As she's retreating, she calls over her shoulder, "If you try to write an article to make up to me, think again. Oldest trick in the book. You're going to have to work harder than that."

Well, there goes that plan.

"But there's a chance?" I call out.

She doesn't say anything, just keeps walking.

But silence is better than a solid no. I'm going to take that as a win.

～

It's past eight o'clock on a Wednesday night, far too late to be knocking on someone's door when they're not expecting you, but that doesn't stop me.

I bounce on my feet, waiting for her to open the door. I'm shocked she let me into the building, but I'm glad for small miracles.

When she opens the door, my breath catches in my chest when I see her, beautiful as ever in a pair of silk pajama shorts and matching top, her hair a wild mess, a bowl of popcorn in her hand.

I forget what I'm doing, until she clears her throat and leans against the doorframe staring at me, silently saying *get on with it*.

Not saying a word, I grab the poster boards I prepared and hold them in front of me, *Love Actually* style. Pulled an idea from one of her favorite movies.

Unfazed, she pops popcorn into her mouth watching the show.

Nerves bloom in me and I start the "slideshow."

Hi June.

Drops board

You look beautiful.

Drop.

I knew you weren't going to be fazed by the compliment, but you do.

Drop.

I came to say I'm sorry.

Drop.

Please give me another chance.

Drop.

(I tried the waterboarding and I couldn't produce enough . . . water-boarding inventory for full effect)

Drop.

So I'm trying this make-up thing again.

Drop.

I miss you.

Drop.

I need you in my life, June.

Drop.

Can I come in?

I smile and try not to choke on my own heart, which seems to be clawing up my throat by the second, with every moment that passes in her silence.

Hope simmers at the base of my spine, pleading that this idea at least gets me inside her apartment. I'm halfway there, getting into the apartment complex was roadblock number one. Roadblock number two is staring at me, shoving popcorn into her mouth, while it looks like a fishhook snagged her eyebrow and is pulling it up toward the sky.

Hmm . . . why do I get the sense this isn't going to go the way I was hoping?

Lifting off the doorframe, mouthful of popcorn, she says, "You're going to have to try harder than that, Waldorf." She moves into her apartment, grips the door, and says, "Your effort to drown in your unborn children is appreciated, though."

I awkwardly wave. "Uh, anytime."

And then she steps back into her apartment and shuts the door.

I glance at the discarded poster boards, my idea in shambles, but my hope has spiked. She said I'm going to have to try harder which means . . . she's receptive to my apology.

One step closer.

~

"June," I say, arms spread, halfway out of the top of a limo, holding a basket of gourmet popcorn rather than flowers.

I've been waiting for the past half hour, sticking half my body out of this limo, waiting for June to leave rehearsals. It seemed like a good idea at first, pulling off the end scene from *Pretty Woman*, but as her rehearsal seemed to run late, I quickly realized what a horrible idea this was, especially after having an empty soda can thrown at me from a rather raucous passerby.

Now I smell like Diet Sprite, my legs are sore from not moving an inch in this death trap of a hole, and I'm sweating in this August heat wearing a three-piece suit.

How did Richard Gere pull off this romantic gesture?

Oh yeah, it was a movie . . .

Horrified, June looks in my direction and stumbles to a stop, her friends in the chorus line all clutching their chests, ooing and ahhing over me.

"Oh my God, he's hot, June," one of the guys says.

"That's The Modern Gentleman?" a girl next to June says. "I'll take you back." She spreads her arms open. "My name is Rebecca, use me as your test subject."

Dear Jesus, no.

Thankfully, June shoos them along and then stands on the sidewalk, staring at me, arms crossed. "What the hell are you doing, Waldorf?"

"June, my girl," I say, trying to get out of the top of the limo, but finding it difficult. I set the basket of popcorn on the top of the roof and hop out of the top, only to have my foot get caught on the ledge of the moon roof and send me barreling down the side, along with the popcorn, and flat onto the sidewalk.

Popcorn spills everywhere.

For the second time since I've known this girl, sidewalk water climbs up my pant leg, and my tailbone breaks my rather ungraceful fall, sending blinding pain up my back.

That is going to bruise.

Yup. Big old bruise.

I quickly pop to my feet, try to gather the popcorn that is not drenched in sidewalk water, and then hold the dilapidated basket out to her. With a smile, I say, "I came bearing apologies and popcorn."

The stern annoyance that was on her face when she first spotted me has disappeared and instead, there is almost—and I mean ALMOST—a lightness about her facial expressions.

I watch as she studies me, her tongue running over the front of her teeth, a smile wanting to tilt up the corners of her lips. I can practically taste the humor that's bubbling up inside of her, but the stone-cold lioness keeps it tamped down as she says, "Better, Waldorf. Better. Not quite there yet, but better."

She takes the popcorn basket from me and starts to walk away.

I call out. "You just got Pretty Womaned."

She looks over her shoulder and calls back, "I don't see you climbing any fire escapes, Mr. Fancy Hair. And that's not an invitation."

Then she spins back around.

Oh I have her . . . I have her right where I want her.

"Have you been drinking?" I ask Roman, who is leaning against the wall, looking less than thrilled to be here.

"What the hell do you think?" Roman asks.

"I think you shouldn't be drunk right before I'm about to pour my heart out to the woman I love."

"Dude," Caden says, gripping my shoulder. "Not going to lie, I've had a few shots too."

"What?" I hiss. "I told you both no drinking. We need to be sharp, on point."

"Have you seen yourself in a mirror?" Roman asks, his voice less than pleased.

I glance down at my bare legs and tube socks. "I look great." I prop my sunglasses down over my eyes and say, "And you both look amazing as well. Now stop making me nervous, I already feel like throwing up."

"I think everyone is going to throw up when they see the three of us." Roman pushes off the wall. "And who do I have to thank for this again?"

"The Jonas Brothers," I say. "Those beautiful geniuses."

"Christ," Roman says.

"I forgot the steps," Caden says in panic.

"You didn't," I snap at him, hopping up and down now. "You're just freaking out. Stop freaking out. WE CAN'T FREAK OUT," I shout just as the manager comes up to me.

"Are you ready, Wes?"

Cue the nausea.

I gulp. "Yup. Ready."

"Okay." He steps through a curtain and speaks into a microphone. "Ladies and gentlemen, we have quite a surprise for you . . ."

Yoo-hoo! Over here!

WAVES FRANTICALLY

Phew, okay. Yeah, it's me, June again.

For this part, let's swing it back over to me, huh?

JUNE

"Are you sad that I'm here with you and not Wes?" my friend Phoebe asks.

I know you don't know who Phoebe is, given she's had maybe one small mention through this entire story, but you can pick your bone with Wes, not me.

If you must know, I met Phoebe in high school. She's a lawyer, stiff as a board, and has a long-time boyfriend, so don't be looking for a story where she's concerned, and she is nothing like the Phoebe from *Friends*. Not even close. But she loves me, I love her, and she's a good voice of reason.

And she knows all about Wes, the good, the bad, and the ugly bruised testicle.

She was the one who made me sit down and read every article Wes wrote about our dating adventure. She was the one who made me realize he wasn't really using me, but telling our story. She was the one who made me realize that even though he was trying to prove his theory right, I disproved it every step of the way. And she was the one who said I'd be stupid not to forgive the man.

Phoebe is good people—even if you don't quite know her, trust me. She's the sidekick every sparkly girl in a rom-com needs in her life.

"I mean, it would have been nice if he was here, but I haven't made it easy on him."

"I wish you had his fall out of the limo roof on video."

I chuckle. "Trust me, me too."

"And you still left the poor man to himself. Brutal, June."

"Left him with some encouraging words." I smile, thinking back to how ridiculous he was yesterday. *You just got Pretty Womaned.* Seriously, he acts like he's this alpha gentleman but in reality, he's a giant doof.

And I love that doof.

Even if I'm mad at him.

We take a seat at one of the reserved tables for the company and I pick up my water just as the manager of the restaurant comes on stage.

"Ladies and gentlemen, we have quite a surprise for you. Please welcome to the stage, The Gents."

Something in my stomach twists as the curtains of Chuck's karaoke diner part, revealing three men all wearing business shirts, no pants, white tube socks, tighty-whities, and black sunglasses.

One of them is bearded.

One of them is far too familiar.

Oh my . . . God.

My hand falls over my mouth as Wes and his friends, Caden and Roman, all sport the classic *Risky Business* Tom Cruise outfit.

White thighs.

Nervous expressions.

Shaky hands gripping the microphones.

Dear God, my heart might explode.

This is Wes's biggest fear and here he is, about to take it on, pantless, no less. I truly think I'm about to get Pretty Womaned. Yesterday was the limo, today is the "fire escape."

The music starts and I instantly recognize the song from one of the nights we were hanging out on Wes's couch, listening to music.

The Jonas Brothers.

Quietly I chuckle, as all three men start bouncing their right leg up and down to the tune of "What a Man Gotta Do."

Do you know the song?

Let's pause for a second.

Grab your phone . . .

Yes, you. Grab your phone and type in "What a Man Gotta Do" by The Jonas Brothers. Give it a quick listen, and you'll see exactly why tears of joy and laughter fill my eyes.

Maybe just play it on repeat right now. I'm serious, it will add to the moment.

Wesley looks up and he sings into the microphone, his voice shaky and nervous, but his confidence pronounced as all three men dance together, Wes taking the lead.

"June, is that your man?" Charlie asks, poking me in the shoulder.

"It is," I answer, keeping my eyes on Wes the entire time.

The chorus kicks in and all three men sing into their microphones and it's the most beautifully awful thing I've ever heard.

They twist, spin, play air guitar.

They do some sort odd version of the Macarena.

They own every last inch of the stage, and the entire restaurant is into it, clapping along with the music, getting into the song, and engaged with Mr. Fancy Hair as he hops off the stage and walks up to me, flipping his sunglasses to the top of his head.

He takes my hand in his, singing the lyrics that ring so incredibly true for this moment, and then lifts me to my feet. His arm wraps around my waist and we sway while everyone around us cheers, mainly my fellow chorus line.

The look in Wes's eyes is pure adoration as he sings off-pitch to me, and it brings me so much joy that tears cascade down my cheeks. There's no stopping them.

And when the song finally finishes, and the room erupts with applause, Wes steps away but still holds my hand, and speaking into the microphone, he says, "June July, what does a man have to do to be locked up by you?"

I wipe at my tears and say, "Exactly that."

He sets the microphone down and brings me closer, gripping both my cheeks. "I'm so fucking sorry, June. I should have been open with you. It was stupid and the epitome of being a dumbass."

A snort bubble comes out of me as I laugh and nod. "It was."

"But I'm here to tell you, even The Modern Gentleman can be a dumbass, but he also can recognize when he's wrong. Lying to you was wrong."

"It was," I answer.

"And it won't happen again. Please tell me I still have a shot at . . . locking you down."

I roll my eyes and place my hand on his chest. "You had to pull the Jonas Brothers into this, didn't you?"

"They spoke to me." He chuckles and sighs. "I love you, June. I love you so fucking hard. Please tell me I didn't completely blow what we have."

My eyes fill up again, happy tears spilling over my cheeks. "You didn't ruin it. You just made it interesting." I stand on my toes and press a light kiss to his lips, only to pull away and say, "I love you, too, Wesley Waldorf, so much . . . but please, for the love of God, put some pants on. Your man thighs are scaring people."

He chuckles and grips my cheeks tighter, bringing me to his mouth and claiming me as his in front of everyone. I melt into him, the press of his hand to my lower back, the feel of his familiar lips whispering over mine. I don't know how it happened, but along this crazy journey of meeting a guy over dog feces, I fell in love with a smart, passionate, and fun-loving man.

He might think he's a gentleman in the streets, an alpha in the sheets, but in real life . . .

Wesley Waldorf Williams is just a plain, old doof.

And I love every doofy part of him.

EPILOGUE

WES

"You were amazing," I say, scooping June into my arms and spinning her around.

"Thank you," she says, pulling away, her stage makeup much heavier than anything I'm used to seeing her in, but she's still beautiful.

"I couldn't take my eyes off you."

"You're only saying that because you're sleeping with me," she coos.

"I'm more than sleeping with you," I say, wiggling my brows. "I'm your main squeeze."

She rolls her eyes. "You were much cooler when I first met you."

"And then you punctured my balls and all that coolness drained out of me."

Her nose scrunches. "Ew, Wes."

I chuckle. "Too far?"

"Just a little. And I didn't puncture you, just bruised."

"Felt like a puncture," I mutter, pressing a kiss to her cheek.

After my brilliant display of karaoke, I won my girl back. How could she not take me back after such a performance? It went viral on HYPE, thanks to our social media marketing manager who filmed the entire thing as the finale of my article.

It was a risky move, in case she didn't take me back, but after I fell out of the limo and saw the look on her face, I knew I was close to getting the girl, I just needed one final moment.

And boy, was it a moment.

After we declared our love for each other, I put pants on because it's true, no one wanted to stare at my man thighs. The boys joined me with their pants and we were invited to the cast party, where Phoebe grilled me over and over about my intentions with June. I had to swear on my belly button—not sure what that was about—that I'd never hurt her again.

I swore.

Because I couldn't imagine ever hurting June, not intentionally, not ever.

She's the girl you hold on to, the once-in-a-lifetime girl, the one you spend your life searching for until she comes along with a one-eared dog and a feisty attitude.

"Juney Bear, there you are," a voice from behind says. I let go of my girl and we both turn toward an older couple. The man has June's eyes and the woman has June's hair.

Her parents.

"Mom, Dad, I didn't know you would be here." She reaches out and gives them both hugs.

"We wouldn't miss this for the world," her mom says. "Grandma would have been so proud."

"Thank you." June holds her heart.

Her dad looks me up and down and says, "This must be Cock-Daddy69."

I blanch as a wave of embarrassment washes over me.

June laughs out loud, grips my arm, and says, "Yes. Mom, Dad, this is Wes or as you know him, CockDaddy69."

"Why do they know me as that?"

June shrugs. "Just seemed more fun that way."

She winks and that right there, that's the reason I love this girl.

"Come on, we should celebrate," June says. "We have tonight to celebrate Wes's book deal and our relationship full of amazing sex."

I choke on my own saliva.

She thumps my back as I say, "Can you tone it down in front of your parents?"

Her mom laughs. "Oh, CockDaddy69, we're just getting started with you."